"Carliz," Valentino made entirely of warnings that her body took as dark, delicious promises—something else she would need to unpack later, when she was alone.

Later, when she knew she'd survived this.

She lifted a hand to stop him. "I'm having your baby," she said. Direct and to the point, and it did not matter what he did with that, not now it was said. "You can do with that information what you will."

And then she finally—*finally*—did the right thing.

She turned on her heel and marched to the front door, leaving him of her own volition.

The Diamond Club

Billion-dollar secrets behind every door...

Welcome to The Diamond Club: the world's most exclusive society, open only to the ten richest men and women alive. The suites are opulent. The service is flawless. And privacy is paramount! You'll never see the details of these billionaires' blistering romances in any of the papers—but you can read all about them right here!

Baby Worth Billions by Lynne Graham

Pregnant Princess Bride by Caitlin Crews

Greek's Forbidden Temptation by Millie Adams

Italian's Stolen Wife by Lorraine Hall

Heir Ultimatum by Michelle Smart

His Runaway Royal by Clare Connelly

Reclaimed with a Ring by Louise Fuller

Stranded and Seduced by Emmy Grayson

All available now!

PREGNANT PRINCESS BRIDE

CAITLIN CREWS

PRESENTS

Harlequin® PRESENTS™

Recycling programs for this product may not exist in your area.

ISBN-13: 978-1-335-93899-2

Pregnant Princess Bride

Copyright © 2024 by Caitlin Crews

For questions and comments about the quality of this book, please contact us at CustomerService@Harlequin.com.

TM and ® are trademarks of Harlequin Enterprises ULC.

 Harlequin Enterprises ULC
22 Adelaide St. West, 41st Floor
Toronto, Ontario M5H 4E3, Canada
www.Harlequin.com

Printed in Lithuania

MIX
Paper | Supporting responsible forestry
FSC® C021394

USA TODAY bestselling, RITA® Award–nominated and critically acclaimed author **Caitlin Crews** has written more than one hundred and thirty books and counting. She has a master's and PhD in English literature, thinks everyone should read more category romance and is always available to discuss her beloved alpha heroes—just ask. She lives in the Pacific Northwest with her comic book–artist husband, is always planning her next trip and will never, ever read all the books in her to-be-read pile. Thank goodness.

Books by Caitlin Crews

Harlequin Presents

Willed to Wed Him
A Secret Heir to Secure His Throne
What Her Sicilian Husband Desires
A Billion-Dollar Heir for Christmas
Wedding Night in the King's Bed
Her Venetian Secret

The Outrageous Accardi Brothers

The Christmas He Claimed the Secretary
The Accidental Accardi Heir

Innocent Stolen Brides

The Desert King's Kidnapped Virgin
The Spaniard's Last-Minute Wife

The Teras Wedding Challenge

A Tycoon Too Wild to Wed

Visit the Author Profile page
at Harlequin.com for more titles.

CHAPTER ONE

PRINCESS CARLIZ HAD never crashed a wedding before.

Not because she was opposed to the idea, in theory, but because she was normally inundated with entirely too many invitations to count. There was usually precious little impetus to go scrounging about for *extra* weddings to attend.

This one, of course, was different.

Her entire life depended on her ability to do what she needed to do at this wedding today, and she knew that if she was to say that to someone—anyone—they would dismiss her and call her needlessly histrionic.

But that didn't make it any less true.

This wedding would always stand as a *before* and *after* moment in her life. It was up to her to make it either a good memory or a deeply sad one, but she knew full well she would be carrying it around forever.

"No pressure, then," she muttered wryly to herself as she boarded the small, sleek watercraft she had hired for her purposes in the Marina di Pisa, tucked there at the mouth of the Arno some ten kilometers from the city famed for its leaning tower.

Carliz had approached this whole enterprise like a

puzzle. She always had liked a good puzzle. And concentrating on the details of how to make it onto a private, tidal island with heaps of security, then into one of the most hyped-up ceremonies of the year when they would most certainly be attempting to keep everyone out, was far more interesting than other things she could have been concentrating on. Like how she felt about the fact that she was doing such a reckless, foolish, and deeply questionable thing in the first place.

But then, Valentino Bonaparte—sometimes called Vale by his friends, which was not how Carliz would describe herself—was the thorniest puzzle of all.

Her curse was that she was determined to solve him, one way or another.

It had been easy enough to secure a boat. She was a princess, the Italian seaside catered to tourists of all descriptions but especially rich ones, and it was nothing at all to whisk her across the stunning blue waters of this part of the Mediterranean Sea. Particularly on a lovely summer day like this. Somewhere between the island of Capraia, renowned for its anchovy fishery, and Elba, better known for the ten months it had housed the exiled Napoleon, sat a small, tidal island that Valentino's family had claimed as theirs for generations.

Carliz wrapped her hair carefully in a silk scarf and sat out in the sea air as the boat cut through the waves, not afraid to imagine herself the heroine on this journey. Bravely striding forth to do what must be done no matter the cost.

It did not matter—at the moment—that she knew that Valentino would not return the favor.

His family like to claim that they were direct descendants of Napoleon himself, but no one took this seriously. She had once heard Valentino say at a party that he rather thought it was an overly imaginative goatherd who had become the first of *his* Bonaparte line. That was all there was on his family's island. Goats, wild oleander, and fortresses on three sides. One belonged to the famously vile Milo Bonaparte, who had raised Valentino and his illegitimate half brother, Aristide, in well-publicized and ongoing conflict. When they had turned eighteen, their father had divided all of the island in two, save the peninsula he lived on, and told his sons to prove which one of them deserved to inherit the rest when he died. Because only one of them could have the greater share.

They had each built their own grand castle on their land. At the other.

For it was well known that the two Bonaparte sons, born on either side of the blanket, had once been great friends but were now mortal enemies. Some speculated it was all down to the inheritance they each hoped to gain, though that made little sense, as both men had made themselves fabulously wealthy in their own right.

But then, Carliz knew all too well that Valentino could exist for years in a state of conflict and feel no compulsion whatever to fix it or even address it. It was like he preferred his own misery. That was another reason that she was taking the extraordinary step she was today, she told herself when the boat landed, and her men helped her alight.

That and the fact that *she* did not like misery at all.

First, though, she had to find the wedding. This was not a large island, as islands went, but it was big enough to be divided into three, each third with enough space to boast its own castle. There was ample opportunity to go to the wrong bit, and then what? She doubted private islands had taxi stands.

She hadn't thought that part through, if she was honest. If her father was still alive, he would no doubt have despaired of her recklessness. Then again, he would have done the same if Carliz had locked herself away in a convent and let the nuns lead her to a higher purpose that might well have involved less of what he'd called his younger daughter's *spiritedness*.

It had never been a compliment.

But Carliz had not gone into the nunnery. Instead, while her serious sister solemnly took the throne after their father's death and their mother had made herself into a walking, talking shrine to his memory, Carliz had done precisely what she pleased.

Because that was the point and privilege of *not* being the heir, to her mind.

Accordingly, she was the first member of her family to attend university in the whole of her tiny kingdom's history. Much less in England, surrounded by commoners. And once she'd graduated with an art degree, Carliz had flirted with the idea of an appropriately bohemian lifestyle, but she soon found that she was too royal to be taken seriously in her preferred medium. She could paint all she liked, and she really did like to paint, but no one could see past her sister's reign when they looked at her works.

Or maybe she was kidding herself, she had no talent whatever, and it was thanks entirely to her sister.

In any case, she had teased Mila—Queen Emilia to everyone else—that it was therefore her obligation and most solemn duty to become the thorn in the proverbial crown.

You can do as you like, her sister had replied in her serene way that was not a reaction to her station. She had always been calm unto her soul. *I only ask that your scandals be entertaining, not embarrassing.*

Carliz had promised. And she always kept her word.

And thus she had sparkled her way all across Europe, from the mountain heights of their tiny little kingdom to Spain's warm beaches, across to the gleaming villas and attendant yachts of the Côte d'Azur. She had skied every hill in Switzerland. She had wandered around the palm trees and wide boulevards of Los Angeles, and spent a season of inner peace and vegan food—not good bedfellows, in her experience—tucked away in a mysterious Malibu canyon.

Your sister indulges you, her mother had said dourly at some point in all this cavorting about, perhaps when Carliz was beginning her first Parisian era. Or maybe it was the second Milan season. It was hard to recall, because it was all couture houses and nights that began after midnight and bled straight on through morning. *But sooner or later you will need to contribute in some way to the crown.*

Surely, Mother, my contribution of joie de vivre *is more than sufficient*, she had replied, not entirely facetiously. *I make Mila laugh.*

You will need to marry well, her mother had thundered at her from behind the shroud she had adopted, the better to look like an early Christian martyr midtorment. She did not laugh. Ever. *Your sister is yet without child. Even you must understand what that means. You have responsibilities, Carliz, whether you like it or not.*

And it was not that Carliz did not want responsibilities. Sometimes she thought she would be much better for them. But there was a restlessness in her. Not a recklessness, as her father had often claimed—it was a kind of yearning. It permeated everything. She was so good at a carefree laugh, a witty comment, the perfect story to set the whole party into gales of laughter. She was terrific at shifting the mood of any room she entered. It was her belief that it was that very restlessness that allowed her to do well at such things, because she was not all on the surface and she did not treat others as if they were, either.

But these were not considered gifts. They were only party tricks. Even though, as far she could tell, the job of the spare princess was to illuminate all the parties she could, her party tricks did not seem to be enough.

Carliz had indulged in vague thoughts about the sort of things she could do. She'd imagined that even though she couldn't think of something intriguing off the top of her head, she could surely find *some* way to be useful instead of merely decorative.

Besides, though she was in no rush to find herself the sort of husband her mother would consider appropriate, Carliz could admit that she was a bit bored with sparkling about hither and yon. A friend of hers suggested charity work, the typical balm for the aimless heiress, which would at least bolster goodwill.

What Carliz had found, instead, was that she truly loved it. She had worked with orphans, at home and abroad, and for the first time in her life had gotten a glimpse—a glimmer—of what it would mean to actually live a life of purpose instead of mere pomp and occasional circumstance.

But then she had met Valentino.

She stopped as she clambered up the rocky beach and let out a breath, because even thinking about him changed the temperature. Of the air. Of the sky. Of her whole body. Even the thought of him made her…silly.

It had been like this from the moment they had met eyes. Met, then held.

Too long for comfort, composure, or anything else the least bit polite.

It had been a charity banquet in Rome. It had been a balmy night and so the banquet had been more or less outside, beneath lights strewn about in the trees and stretching between the old walls to create a ceiling in the old ruin, so that everything was cast in a warm, bright glow.

Everything except him.

He was breathtaking. Thick dark hair, a sensually stern mouth, and eyes like a faded blue sky set against his olive coloring to swoon-worthy effect.

And yet there was something ruthless in the cut of him. The blade of his nose, the slice of his cheekbones, the intense athleticism of his form that was obvious even in the exquisite bespoke suit he'd worn that night.

Carliz had felt drawn to him as surely as if he'd wrapped his arms around her and hauled her to him.

Oh, how she wished he had.

She had worn red that night. And red was how she'd felt—seared through, set alight, and made new.

She remembered catching his gaze the way she had, and then, in the next moment, finding herself in his arms. As if it had happened that way, in an instant. As if neither one of them had moved at all. As if fate had taken a hand and thrown them together, from one end of a crowded event into the center of a packed dance floor.

That was impossible. She knew that. One of them must have moved toward the other. There must have been some understanding, some communication—but if so, it was lost to her. All she recalled was that searing glance.

She could still *feel* it. She felt it *all the time*.

And then, better still, the exquisite beauty and agony of being in his arms.

They hadn't spoken. It was too intense, too overwhelming.

And she knew this had not been in her head alone. For one, she was not given to such flights of fancy. And for another, she'd seen it on his face. That stark wonder. And something else—that same alarm she could feel in her, too, that *anything* could sweep through them like this.

Because things like this could not be real.

There was no such thing as love at first sight. Everyone knew it.

Tell me your name, he had said at last, and they had both reacted to that.

She had shivered, because his voice seemed to be a part of her already, moving deep within her, changing her and claiming her. And she had shivered again when his eyes had moved to track the goose bumps that rose up, then trailed down the line of her neck, then out across her bare shoulders.

Carliz, she had managed somehow, to say. *Princess Carliz of the Kingdom of Las Sosegadas.*

I am Valentino, he had replied.

And later, she would find herself tempted to analyze that. To suspect that he had deliberately not told her his surname and puzzle over the fact that he had also not offered her that nickname of his, but in her brighter moments she knew better. Neither one of them had been in possession of any defenses in that moment. It would have been better if they had.

It would have been easier, then and now.

After the dance had ended, he'd drawn her off the dance floor, and they had stood there, too full of each other to breathe. Too…altered.

She could remember the amazement on his face. That same wonder she could feel sparking within her. She remembered the way he'd led her through the party when he could bring himself to move, in a way that should have made a scene, given who they were, though no one afterward had remarked on it.

To her it was so obvious, this thing that had blown up between them. So blatantly sensual. So impossibly carnal.

So *right*.

When they reached the shadows outside the ruin, at

last, he had backed her against the nearest remnant of a wall and looked down into her eyes.

Carliz, he had said, as if her name on his tongue was an anguish all its own. *Carliz, this is not who I am.*

She hadn't spoken. She'd felt...almost choked by the intensity of that moment. His gaze on her. Her very real sense that she had fallen off a cliff from all that she knew and there was only this freefall, now. That there was no way out. No going back. No fixing whatever this was.

No story she could tell or witticism she could offer that would make this any less than it was.

So instead, following an urge she could hardly name, she had lifted up her hands and traced those sensually harsh lines of his stunning face. She had made a soft noise when she'd touched him, when the heat of him seemed to rush through her like its own, deep roar.

His skin was scalding to the touch. His brows were a symphony, a weapon.

And when she'd moved her fingertips over that austere, demanding mouth of his, he'd opened his lips and enveloped her fingers with all of that terrible, wonderful heat. And she had learned things about herself, then.

Dark, magical things.

Too many things to name, cascading through her all at once, and all of them lessons of heat and wonder, longing and desire.

Inexorably and not nearly fast enough, one of his hands had found its way to the nape of her neck and held her there.

And she'd known he was going to kiss her.

She had felt as if she'd been waiting the whole of her life to kiss him back.

And when he'd lowered his face to hers and claimed her mouth with his, she was certain she had waited an eternity.

For then Carliz was born anew.

Because he kissed like wonder. And with one stroke of his tongue after the next, he wrote his name indelibly on her heart. She kissed him back in the same way, the heat and marvel reaching a crescendo all its own.

When he'd pulled back, they were both shaking.

And then, as she'd watched him and panted out her need and frustration that they were not *still* kissing, Valentino had stepped back. He had squeezed his eyes shut. He had rubbed his hands over his face and made a sound that she could only describe as pure anguish.

She had felt it in her own gut, like a dagger thrust in deep.

This cannot happen, he had told her.

Carliz had sighed a little. *I think it already has.*

This cannot happen, he had said again, and he had fixed the dark world of his eyes on her. *This will not happen.*

And she would never understand—to this day, she could not understand—how he had turned as sharply as he did, then walked away and left her there, as if what had happened between them was a daydream. As if it had not happened at all.

She didn't follow him that night. She couldn't. She had stayed where she was, clutching onto that wall as if without it she might topple off the planet and lose herself amongst the stars forever.

But eventually, she had gotten her legs beneath her again.

Eventually she had learned how to breathe as if breath was new.

And when she did, she went to war.

Carliz reminded herself of that now as she made her way through a bit of a hedge and found herself on a brightly lit lane, where many exquisite-looking people in fancy dress were walking along, all headed toward the grand, sprawling house on the hill above them.

Or more precisely, she realized as she slipped into the procession as demurely as possible, toward the small chapel that sat tucked in at the foot of the hill, with a view over the sea she'd only just crossed.

A pretty place for a wedding, she thought. And then she congratulated herself on how clinical that thought was, as if everything in her body didn't rise up to reject it. There were rooms in the house up above, with windows that looked straight down at the procession toward the chapel, and she couldn't help but wonder if he was there now. Watching. Waiting.

Preparing to marry a woman who wasn't her.

Carliz glanced up, then forced herself to stop. And as she walked the rest of the way, she kept her scarf as much over her face as she could and kept her gaze toward the ground, because she did not wish to be recognized. Not yet.

She had spent the past three years paparazzi-ing herself at Valentino Bonaparte. Who had not been able to avoid her entirely, though he had not touched her again. Still, every time their gazes locked it was like fireworks, and he hated her for that.

Or maybe it was that he hated that she would not let it go.

Though Carliz thought that of the two of them, she was the one who really ought to have hated him. For experiencing what she had that night, then walking away. For kissing her like that, as if no other woman would ever exist but her, and as if he could not live without her.

And then having the audacity to go ahead and do just that.

She had spent two years making the relationship she hadn't actually had with him into one of the biggest scandals in Europe. All it took was a whisper to this tabloid, an anonymous tip to another. Making sure she was spotted leaving places he had been. Making sure that it looked as if she was trying to hide from the cameras while she did it.

After all, speculation was often better than any real story could ever be.

Then he had announced his engagement to a blameless, spotless heiress of indisputably high character.

Carliz did not like to think about that particular day. It had been a dark one.

Even her sister had called, filled with sympathy and endless concern…though more because Mila was worried about what Carliz might do, Carliz was aware. Less about the state of Carliz's heart.

Not the Carliz could tell anyone about the *actual* state of her heart.

Once again, she hadn't thought things through. Everybody thought that she and Valentino had been involved in a torrid affair. Since she was chiefly known for her sparkling and not her charitable works, the narrative had tended toward praising Valentino for keeping his side of the street scrupulously clean while offering very thinly veiled jabs at Carliz for being such a mess in public.

She had thought it was all fun and games. That, at the very least, it would inspire Valentino to confront her himself.

But he had declined.

And so she didn't see him again until after his engagement. When they had both inadvertently turned up at the same birthday party for another European royal, who Valentino knew from his own time at university. Or perhaps it was from that desperately fancy club everyone knew he was a part of, so exclusive that people spoke of it in whispers—even when the people that they were speaking to had no idea it existed.

This time there had been no dancing. He was an engaged man and it was clear he did not intend there to be any scandal attached to him, or to his lovely, worthy intended who Carliz did her best not to loathe simply because *she existed*.

Nonetheless, thanks to Carliz's antics, there were entirely too many eyes watching the two of them as they came face-to-face at that party.

I hope you are satisfied with yourself, Valentino had said, a banked storm in those faded blue eyes and censure all over his face.

As satisfied as I imagine you are with yourself, she had replied, with a smile for the onlookers. *A thousand congratulations on your future happiness, Valentino.*

Saying his name to him washed through him, its own wave. She could see it. She could feel its echo inside her own bones.

That storm in his gaze had intensified.

I owe you no obligation, he had shot back. *I told you. Whatever this is, it cannot happen. I* told you *this.*

It makes no sense to me, she had said, and there was too much *feeling* in her voice. There was too much raw emotion all over her, spilling out everywhere. She knew it but she couldn't seem to keep it within.

We should never have met, he had told her, and then he had once again walked away.

Carliz had not even had to go out and drum up the headlines that had greeted her the next day. Because she'd created the monster and now it fed itself. The papers were full of speculation about their tense meeting. About their lost love.

About this untenable situation she had created for herself.

About this man who she knew full well felt as she did, but refused to accept it. And refused even further to *do* anything about it.

Carliz had resolved to get over him. To put that lightning strike of a meeting behind her and move on.

But then she'd seen him one more time.

She had not been supposed to be there. She couldn't remember the name of the event, only that it took place in a forlorn castle somewhere in England, carefully refurbished but still little more than a lonely beacon over a remote and barren landscape. Like a lighthouse standing over a rocky shore where no ships sailed.

She had come in the night before after attempting to exhaust herself with literal whirlwinds of the sort of activities that she'd used to find such fun. She'd gone on a mad tour from the Pacific Islands to Rio de Janeiro to Barcelona, all to forget about Valentino Bonaparte. She had been sandy and salty, her ears still ringing from too much music and her whole body in need of a month's rest after all of that dancing.

And so she had slept through the day and into the next night with the party already carrying on in the castle's ancient keep below. When she'd woken up she'd felt inside out and in no fit state to interact with anyone.

Carliz was very good at pulling the pieces together, no matter her actual state. She had always been good at it. A little bit of makeup and she was fine. She was well. A pretty dress and she was giddy and happy, and whatever else she was required to be at any given time.

But that night, she had felt pale with exhaustion. And not simply the kind that sleeping could cure. Her heart was too heavy. She had begun to think that he was right. That they should never have met.

If they had never met, she would never have known.

If she hadn't known, she would not have to suffer like this.

She could not, somehow, find it in her to buck up, put on her party face, and go out there where people would expect her to sparkle the way she always did.

Carliz went to her window instead to look out over

the party below, and that was when she saw that he was there.

It was a glory and misery to see him, to feel that electricity—that same old lightning bolt—and yet to know that it was meaningless. She thought it was so unjust that it was possible to feel that way about someone and have it mean so little. To know, against her will, that it was possible to fall for someone like this and also to know that it was futile.

She had been so sure that she could convince him to take the chance. She had been so positive that he would come around.

Maybe the real trouble was that Carliz was not accustomed to failures. Because she did not set herself up with true challenges, perhaps. Because she did not ask much of herself. She knew that was what some would say.

Or maybe, she thought then, it was just she was heartbroken. And she would remain heartbroken. She would never be able to explain it to anyone else, because they wouldn't believe her if she told the truth and she couldn't bring herself to actually tell someone a lie. What the papers said, she couldn't control. She could only insinuate, then fail to correct their assumptions, and they had drawn their own conclusions.

But now…now she was simply going to have to live with this.

So she watched him from her window, aware that he would not be pleased if he caught her at it. That he would prefer to pretend she did not exist at all, and if she did, that they did not recognize each other.

She was going to have to live with that, too. And

maybe, someday, learn how to convince herself that she couldn't recognize him after all.

Carliz told herself that it was a farewell. His wedding was in a handful of months and that would be that. Because her scandals had only ever been entertaining, as her sister had requested. They could not involve a married man. They would not.

She couldn't even allow herself to be the fake lover of a married man. It would be too cruel to his wife. Too unnecessarily vicious when the truth was, it would only be more acrobatics around the same heartbreak.

So she stood there instead and watched him as he commanded space around him. As others flocked to him, the way they always did.

She told herself this would have to do, and then she would surrender herself to whatever her mother thought was necessary to do her duty. She saw no reason to delay the inevitable, not now.

That should have been the end of it. She was sure that it would have been.

Except as she watched, Valentino stepped away from the rest of the crowd. He stood on the edge of the keep, half in shadow, and seemed to do nothing at all but breathe.

She found herself pressed up against the window, watching him avidly, because he didn't know she was here. No one did. He didn't know she could see him, that in fact, she might be the only one at the party who could.

There was no way he could know that she was the only one who saw the way he let his eyes drift shut for the barest moment, as a look as close to grief as any she had ever seen crossed over his face.

It was the exact same look she had seen once before.

When he had stepped away from her after that kiss. In that moment before he told her that nothing could happen between them.

And in that moment, she knew. Valentino was not resigned to this course he had taken. He was not happy about his upcoming wedding.

This, tragically, meant that Carliz had no choice.

At first she'd thought it would be that very night. She'd pulled herself together, had gone downstairs, yet by the time she made it to the party he had already left. And later she'd read in the papers that they had planned it that way, the two of them. Ex-lovers, according to the tabloids, who clearly could not stand to be in the same room with each other.

If only, she had thought sourly. Instead, she was an ex-lover who had never been a lover at all, and how unfair was that?

That was when she'd begun planning this puzzle.

Carliz knew full well that this was her last chance. Her only chance. Even she could only beat her head against the same brick wall for so long. She slipped into the lovely, airy chapel with the rest of the guests, keeping her eyes demurely lowered as she took a seat in one of the pews toward the back.

Here, too, she hadn't planned exactly what she would do. She was hoping the perfect solution would come to her. She knew that there was always the option of standing up in the middle of the ceremony, assuming that was something they did here. Not that she was entirely certain that her objection would count. Besides, she couldn't help but feel that standing up like that would be seen as an act of violence, and she wasn't sure she wanted to deal with the fallout of such a dramatic scene.

On the other hand, waiting for Valentino to come to his senses hadn't worked either.

It had done the exact opposite of working, in fact.

And so she sat, feeling overly warm and more than a little bit distressed, wondering if she was *truly* prepared to put herself beyond the pale like that. It was one thing when it was nothing but a few headlines in the outrageously and notably untrue tabloids. There were people here, however. People who would watch and witness whatever it was she did here. People who would always know that Carliz de Las Sosegadas was the sort of person who would disrupt another woman's wedding.

Her sister would never forgive her. It was precisely the sort of embarrassing event that she had asked Carliz to avoid.

Carliz was not big on prayer, but she found herself casting a few missives upward, asking for a better option.

She waited and she waited. The people around her began to fidget in their seats, and the low murmur of speculation began to get louder.

Until, eventually, a door opened toward the front of the chapel and a man stepped in. She tensed, but knew in the next moment that it was not Valentino. This was a shorter man, rounder. He marched into the middle of the altar, and bowed slightly to the assembly.

"I regret to inform you all that the wedding will not be going forward as planned," he said. "Please accept the deepest apologies for having come all this way. A fleet of boats has been called into ferry you all back to the mainland as the tide is yet high. Good day."

All around, the murmurs broke into full-throated speculation. Excited whispers became nervous laughter, and Carliz was fairly certain she could hear her name in the comments—though no one had spotted her here.

She felt a bit of shame all the same, if she was honest.

But she still didn't move, because her mind was racing. And the worst part of all was that here she was, sitting in a chapel where a wedding had just been called off and she suspected that she would be named as a reason for that decision. She couldn't argue it. She had put herself in that position and more, she had done so all by herself.

Yet inside her, she felt the faintest, tiniest, strangest little sliver of hope.

And so, when everyone else left the chapel, she followed. She held that scarf around her face, looking around to make sure that no one was monitoring her, and as the rest of the guests made their way to the water, Carliz headed to the big house on the hill—and Valentino—instead.

CHAPTER TWO

WHEN THE DOOR to his bedchamber opened without permission, Valentino Bonaparte tried to convince himself that the woman who appeared before him like an apparition was little more than a daydream, but he knew better.

Valentino was many things, many of them apparently unpardonably foolish, but he had not stooped to lying to himself. Not yet.

Though there were a great many hours left in this already cursed day. Given what had already occurred—something he would have assumed was impossible—he could not rule anything out.

"You cannot possibly be here," he told the woman who stood there in the doorway. The doorway to his bedroom, a place where she had spent entirely too much time—if only in the dreams he preferred to act as if he did not have.

She did not smile. Not quite. "And yet I am."

He turned fully around, putting his back to the window where he had stood all this while. First waiting for the guests to arrive so the task of his wedding could be completed in an orderly fashion. Then watching them all leave in the wake of his man's announcement.

There was no doubt that the world would soon know that Valentino's deliberately provocative half brother had upped the ante by stealing his bride out from under his nose and on the day of the wedding, but he had not felt that *he* needed to announce it.

It was enough, surely, to cancel the entire affair.

And now Carliz was here. Without invitation.

As always.

He took a moment to study her as she stood there, framed by the open doorway, aware that he was responding to her the way he always did. His chest felt tight. His blood ran hot. His sex was hard.

Time did not improve his reaction to this woman. Distance did not diminish it.

She had been bothersome from the moment they'd met.

Today she was dressed in what looked like a selection of flowing scarves, including one draped over her head. As if she thought anything could conceal her. But Valentino would know her anywhere.

Carliz was drawn in regal lines, from her smooth brow to her aquiline nose to the willowy form she inhabited with a certain, specific grace that was entirely her own—and set every part of him alight. She was the sort of woman who gave the impression of being forever languid, when a closer inspection always revealed that there was nothing languid about the way she carried herself. Princess Carliz was the walking embodiment of what might happen if a lightning bolt turned itself human, wrapped itself in supple flesh, and created storms wherever she went.

He knew the way she smelt. A faint hint of spice, so faint that when he had been close to her—on two very dangerous occasions—he had wanted nothing so much as to bury his face in her neck, breathe her in until that scent was a part of him, and then find every part of her body, every secret space, where he might lose himself in her more fully.

Sometimes he dreamed that scent and woke, alone and furious all over again.

Valentino knew the way she tasted, a mad heat that he had spent years acting as if he could not recall. Or had forgotten. Or had never found compelling in the first place.

He had never had another choice. The only other option was chaos, and it was clear to him that the events of the day made it more than obvious that the role of chaos agent in the Bonaparte family was already taken.

But he remembered the way Carliz had looked at him after that ill-advised kiss, her gaze ripe with a kind of wonder, bright with stars, and impossible. That was what he knew to be true of this woman above all else.

She was impossible.

Then again, this was a day already filled with impossible things. What was one more?

"Did you do this?" he asked her quietly.

She moved further into the room, pushing the scarf that must have covered her face back so he could see the soft, burnished gleam of her hair—not quite blond, not quite red, but something that danced between the two and flirted with shades of brown besides. He could not see which of the layers she wore were wraps or scarves and which might suggest the presence of a dress—and Valentino thought he might go mad with wondering. With the way the soft fabric moved against her body, concealing more than it revealed, and yet making him hunger to see the rest.

To taste her at last. Everywhere.

He suspected she was fully aware of his reaction. That she had planned for it, in fact, and he did not want that image in his head—of Carliz gauging her own feminine power in a mirror, fully knowing what it would do to him.

It had been a point of agony for him in these past years that she knew him far better than she should. Whatever it was that had exploded between them that cursed night, she had been able to use it to her advantage. Or so it seemed to him, because he could find nothing at all advantageous in the way this woman affected him.

But he was not the sort of man who cried mercy.

"I suppose I can glean from that question that you are not the one who called off your own wedding," she was saying.

He thought she would cross to him, but instead she wandered through the room instead, and he wondered if she knew that he would never be able to sleep well in here again. Not without remembering the way she drifted so close to the end of the bed, letting her hand dance over the coverlet. Not without getting that scent of hers everywhere, like the faintest shower of cinnamon powder on everything.

Valentino would see her ghost here, forever, gazing

at the art on his walls then looking past him toward the view of the rest of the island, carefully situated to show neither his father nor his brother's houses. He preferred to act as if he was the only Bonaparte here, as he was the only one concerned with the family legacy, and had built his house to make certain it seemed that way while he was here.

It was only after Carliz had taken in all these things, all the tiny details that made up his life—a life he did not wish for her to know anything about—that she turned back to look at him once more.

Her gaze, as always, was direct. Knowing. Too steady for his own good.

Once she was gone, Valentino knew that he would be tormented by this moment. That he would spend un-countable hours seeking out her scent when it could not possibly linger here. When he would make sure the staff scoured this room to make certain it could not.

Even now, he wanted to lean closer, to inhale deeply, to reach out and put his hands on her—

Weary as he was of the virtue that had so far gotten him precisely nothing in this life, Valentino clung to it.

He did not close the space between them. Because he knew better. He did not get his hands on her, nor in-dulge himself by finding out what, exactly, was beneath those dancing, flowing scarves. If it was only the hint of her bare skin that he saw, every time she breathed, or if it was truly possible that any sudden movement might send all of that fabric sliding to the floor.

You do not need to know, he told himself with a clenched sort of piety.

"I did not call off the wedding," Valentino told her, before he forgot that he ought to make this a conversation and not another staring match with all of these unnecessary *other things* he did not intend to do anything about. "The bride was thoughtful enough to send a message that she would not be attending the festivities, so canceling the ceremony seemed a prudent next step."

It had not been a message, as such. It had been a report from his security detail that his bride had run off to the other side of the island, clad in her wedding dress, in the company of none other than Aristide.

Rumor has it he married her, signor, his man had informed him a shockingly short while later. Before the guests had even left the chapel.

The thought of his half brother filled him with the usual roar of fury and pain, old grudges, and worse still, those persistent memories of the friendship they'd had. Before they knew who they really were to each other. Before the truth had come out.

Before Valentino had lost not only his mother, but his inheritance. And also his relationship with the housekeeper who had been sleeping with his father all along while treating Valentino as if he was also her son. Ginevra, the housekeeper he had viewed as family.

And Aristide himself.

The friend he had considered a brother until it turned out he really *was* his brother, and that ruined everything.

On a philosophical level, Valentino had no idea why it hadn't been obvious to him from the start that Aristide would ruin even this. A wedding that should not have registered on his brother's radar, as Valentino very much doubted that matrimony interested the profligate, careless Aristide in the least.

All Aristide ever cared about was making things difficult for the brother from whom he had already taken so much.

He excelled in it.

Luckily, Valentino thought now, as he often did, *I care only and ever about one thing.*

Aristide could tarnish his own name all he liked— but Valentino embodied the family legacy. He *was* the Bonaparte tradition, despite his father's best efforts and his brother's many antics. *He* would not tarnish.

If anything, this wedding nonsense would only make Valentino look better by contrast. The very picture of duty and quiet resignation in the face of more unsavory behavior from the usual suspects.

Really, he should thank Aristide for making the case himself so airtight. Though he knew he would not. That he would die first, in fact.

"Well," said Princess Carliz, looking at him with those curious eyes of hers that made him think of treasure chests and ancient castles, the kind of things that ran in her blood back through the ages.

"Well?" he echoed.

And it was then, as Valentino heard the edge in his own voice, that he realized two things.

One, that he had not already called to have her removed, which he would like to put down to the demands of this moment—but he could not pretend that he was emotional about this. Not in the way one might expect a jilted groom to be. He was annoyed, yes. He did not like the mess of this or the fact he knew that he would be required to do some cleanup. He also did not care to have his plans altered.

But two, and more critically, it only just now occurred to him that he and Carliz were…alone.

All alone, here in his bedchamber, where no one else would dare set foot without his express permission.

That thing in him that he had gone to such lengths to keep at bay, to keep at arm's length, to keep *away* from beat hot and hard.

"I hope you don't expect my sympathies." Carliz looked at him with an expression he'd seen before. It was that *knowing* look of hers that he disliked intensely. Because she should not know him. She should not know a single thing about him. They were strangers. Except, of course, that was not precisely true—though it should have been. And he could not understand why it was that this woman got to him in ways no one else ever had. In ways he could not allow. "I don't know why you were marrying the poor girl in the first place."

"I can assure you that there is nothing poor about her."

Carliz waved an impatient hand. "Do not bore me with some tedious dissertation on your dynastic responsibilities, please. There is no possible way that you have heard more on that score that I have over the years. My sister's potential husband search requires a committee to splice together the perfect bloodlines that appeal to my mother's European sensibilities, my sister's refinement and consequence, and what the palace considers appropriate advertising for the next generation of the modern kingdom. If they could get away with a lab experiment and a selection of petri dishes, I believe they would."

"The bride may have had second thoughts," Valentino said, lifting his shoulder in the barest shrug. And he did not choose to ask himself why it was that he was so happy to let Carliz think he was nonchalant about this. Before she'd walked into the room, he had been as close to irate as he allowed himself to become—though always with the strictest control. He did not particularly wish to figure out why he did not want her to know that. "Luckily, I do not require lab experiments in petri dishes, only a certain level of respectability. I am sure she will be easily replaced."

"How tempting for the next figurine you tote to the altar." Carliz's voice was scathing, something she very clearly did not mind if he knew. "If only I, too, could be a nameless puzzle piece for you to move about at will, easily and often duplicated, exchanged, then soon enough forgotten."

And for the first time since he'd woken up this morning, filled with the dark resolve that had gotten him into this position in the first place and fully prepared to execute his duty no matter what, Valentino found himself feeling…something a whole lot like *good*.

There was no other way to explain the sudden lightness he could feel in him after so long holding up the weight of this heaviness he'd brought upon himself. Because despite what his wretched father had done—from parading his mistress beneath his wife's nose and thereby, eventually, causing his wife's death to all the years of pitting his legitimate son against his bastard for his own entertainment—Valentino had always been conscious of his place. Of who he was. Who he would always be, no matter what games his father played. No matter what became of his inheritance.

He was still and ever Valentino Bonaparte, the one and only true heir to his family's legacy. It was still incumbent upon him to be the Bonaparte he wished to see in the world. Not like his reckless half brother, certainly. And certainly nothing like his cruel father.

There had been others before Milo, and it was Valentino's job to make certain that there would be more after him. Men like his grandfather, dignified and reserved, and filled with distaste for the sort of person Milo had become. There had been the uncles that Milo had always hated, mostly because they didn't approve of him. There had been the older one, Vincenzo, the original heir. He had been a stalwart man in his own father's style, all that was intelligent and fair-minded. But he had died, taken abruptly when he was in his twenties, long before he'd had the chance to secure his legacy.

It was the youngest brother in the family, Bruno, who had told Valentino stories about the lost heir to the Bonaparte fortune. Uncle Bruno, who had been deeply revolted by Milo for most of his life and had renounced the family entirely when he'd moved to America and married his long-term partner. Severing all ties in his wake.

Valentino had always been keenly aware that if only the sainted Vincenzo had married and secured the family line earlier rather than later, so much of what had happened after could have been averted.

He had felt as if a clock were always ticking in him as he'd set about securing his own fortune, so that he would never, ever be dependent upon his father's cruel whims. It had been a relief to decide that he was finally ready and then to move forward as swiftly as possible. His requirements for a wife were quite simple, after all. He wanted someone practical and biddable. His mother had been neither of those things, and look at where she had ended up. His mother had been emotional. She had fancied herself in love with Milo, she had suffered for it, and Milo had used that love shamelessly.

Valentino had always been clear on that score after watching the many disasters of his family unfold before him. There would be no love where he was concerned. Love cursed whoever it touched. Love corroded and destroyed.

Love was, at best, a catastrophic disaster.

Love, apparently, was what kept Ginevra, the housekeeper of his youth and long his father's lover, still at her job tending to the original house on the estate and Milo himself even though her own son had done shockingly well for himself and should have been more than able to support her.

He could not think of a better warning against love than the two women who had actually loved a monster like Milo Bonaparte. His mother had died. Ginevra toiled on. None of them were happy, nor ever would be.

With all of that in mind, Valentino had decided that Francesca Campo fit the bill nicely. She had been so biddable that she had nearly disappeared in the middle

of conversations. It was true that he had found her boring, but he had thought that was a positive.

After all, if he'd wanted a lightning bolt, he'd known
right where to find one.

And right now, said lightning bolt was advancing
upon him.

"Do you know why I am here?" she was demanding,
with all her usual delicacy.

Which was to say, none. For a princess, she was astonishingly direct.

"Somehow I doubt it was to offer your felicitations,"
he murmured, watching those scarves dance and flow as
she moved, damn her. "Likely that is the reason you're
not invited."

"I had to sneak onto this island," she told him. "I
had to crash your wedding, the only event of any sig-
nificance that I have not been invited to in as long as I
can recall."

"Perhaps you have confused reality and fantasy yet
again," he said coolly, though nothing in him was cool.
It was all fire and the dark. The dangerous, envelop-
ing dark. "Is it possible that you forgot, once more, that
we have no relationship, you and I? Did you perhaps
tell yourself a different story so often that you forgot
it was a lie?"

"We might not have had the wild affair the papers
think we did," she said, coming to stand directly before
him, that gaze of hers trained on him. "But this is not
a *lie*, Valentino. And I don't need you to tell the truth
about it. I know the truth."

"What is it you think you know, *Principessa*?" he

asked, though he knew better. He knew this was not a conversation he should allow. He had made certain, for years, that it could not take place. There was no reason to stop now. But he could not seem to keep himself from it. "What is it you imagine this is?"

She opened her mouth as if to answer him, but then stopped. And he knew too much about her for his own good, though he had vowed to himself that he would pretend they had never met. Still, he had found himself accidentally finding his way to articles, here and there. Not simply the usual tabloid fodder that trailed about after her, but the few actual, interesting discussions of who she was, mostly in relation to her sister, Queen Emilia of Las Sosegadas, a tiny little jewel of a kingdom tucked away in the mountains between France and Spain.

And even then, he had felt as if every sentence he'd read had been confirmation of something he already knew from their brief, electric meetings. He could see that she was clever. It was the way she looked at him, and right through him, when no one else had ever seemed particularly capable of that.

No one, that was, except his brother—but he chose not to focus on that twisted, tortuous relationship.

Carliz was beautiful, yes, but he had seen her when she was not putting on that act of hers. Not that she was *not* bright and glorious, drawing everyone near. She was all of that, but she was also more. She was not *only* that gleaming, laughing version of herself, and even though the moments they had spent together did not add up to even an hour, he had seen more of her than the whole of the world.

He told himself that was a curse, but it felt more like a blessing.

"I have a better idea," she said now, studying him. "Why don't you tell me what this is?"

"I have told you. Repeatedly." But he would do so again, because he needed to hear it too. "It is nothing. It can only be nothing. It will never be anything else."

"That does not sound like nothing." She shook her head. "And if it was really nothing, I feel certain you would already have had me removed from this room. Ejected from the grounds of your estate. Or thrown in jail like any other sad little stalker. But that's not what I am, is it?"

Valentino was surprised that there was the urge in him to agree with her. To say the unsayable things. To throw himself off a cliff, here and now. He did not know how he managed to keep himself from giving in to it. That was how strong it was. "I understand what you want me to say. But that doesn't mean I will say it."

"Of course not. Because if you said it, then you could no longer hide away in all your denial. And then what would you do?"

And Valentino laughed. It was a rusty sound, because he was not a particularly joyful or typically amused person. He was a man of strict compartments. Only his mother and his brother had ever called him by his full name, and he liked it that way. Because now that his mother was dead, it was only his greatest enemy who called him Valentino.

To the rest of the world, he was Vale. It made things very easy for him. Anyone who called him by the nickname knew only the performance he put on, not him.

But Carliz called him Valentino. Worse, he had told her to. He had given her that name himself, when he never did such a thing. He always handed out his nickname, so he could file the people who used it into the appropriate spaces.

"I saw you in Paris not long ago," he told her. "I was there on business. You were there to make a scene."

"I would say I remember," she replied, looking unrepentant. "But that would be a lie."

"I remember well enough. You were there with the usual entourage. Taking over the restaurant, spilling out into the streets." He had not expected to see her. He had been shocked she had somehow not felt the weight of his stare, or simply *felt* his presence, and he didn't like what that said about him. "You were laughing and making merry though it was clear to me that you were empty inside."

"But have you not heard? I am always empty inside. That is one of the foremost qualities about me that people admire." She leaned closer, and he was hit with that spice and a hint of silk. "The emptier I am, the more they can imagine me however they like. It makes for a lovely sparkle, and I am nothing if not *sparkly*. Really, it is a public service."

"I told myself I was not following you," he said, not sure why he was telling her this. Not sure why he was admitting to this fault in his character. "I was merely walking back along the same boulevard. And you had no idea that I was there. You were simply careening this way and that in a Parisian night, heedless of your surroundings."

"I pay a security detail a great deal of money to make certain that I can be as heedless as I like, whenever I like." Though Carliz smiled, wryly. "It is more honest to say that the crown pays, because as my sister has pointed out many times, she would be the one called upon to pay a ransom for anything truly upsetting to befall me. Still. I was perfectly safe." Again she studied him again. "But you were not concerned about my safety, were you?"

"You looked so lost, Carliz," he told her, and maybe he knew she would react to that. That she would suck in a breath. "That was when I decided to forgive you for all the lies you have told about the two of us over the years. I doubt you knew any better." He leaned in, just a little, the better to stick in the knife. "Just a lost little princess, stumbling around Europe, making messes for her sister to clean up."

He saw something flash in her eyes, but in the next moment, she laughed. And this was not that sparkly laugh of hers that she trotted out in front of the cameras. Or for her shallow little friends' mobile phones. This was a low sort of laugh, warm and deep.

It moved in him like the kind of fine bourbon he only allowed himself seldomly.

"It's not going to work," she told him. "I can't be shamed. Though you are welcome to try, if you like. Everyone does."

"Princess," he said from between his teeth, as if she

was the one needling him when he had just sunk a knife in, deep. And on purpose. "This has been a challenging day. I am now embroiled in a scandal not of my own making and you are here, right in the middle of it. It makes me wonder what level of collusion there has been between you and my brother."

She looked intrigued by that. "I absolutely would have colluded with your brother. But I didn't think of it."

"When I leave this room I will have to pick up the pieces, yet again, from one more disaster not of my making." Valentino let out his own laugh then, but this time it was nothing but bleak. "I cannot even blame my brother. He has always behaved as badly as possible, I assume to live down to the expectations placed upon him. I cannot blame my would-be bride, for it is not as if she truly betrayed me. That would require an emotional connection we never had. But you are something else again. I find it is easy enough to blame you."

"You can blame me all you want," Carliz threw right back at him.

She stepped even closer, and now it was dangerous. They were barely a breath apart. Her scent was all around him, and he could feel her heat, too, and it would not even require a decision to reach out for her. He could simply exhale—

"Good," Valentino growled. "Because I intend to blame you for everything. Thoroughly."

"Please do," she dared him. "At last."

And maybe he needed that decision to be made, even if she was the one to make it. Either way, he finally shrugged off that leash he'd had wrapped tight around his own neck since he'd first laid eyes on her in Rome. After all this time, after letting it choke him for years, he finally just…cut the chain.

Because this day of all days, Valentino thought he might as well do the thing he was already accused of doing. He might as well have *one taste* since he had already paid for it in the press. Over and over again. And would likely continue paying for it after today.

And besides, he had always rather liked a lightning storm.

Maybe he had needed a disaster of this magnitude to admit it.

Valentino reached out and put his hands on her body, the silk of those scarves and the heat of her skin beneath. Then he drew her closer still, so that body of hers was pressed against his chest the way he woke up remembering, sometimes.

This was like that night, but much, much better.

Because when he kissed his maddening princess this time, he had no intention of stopping.

CHAPTER THREE

CARLIZ HAD SPENT a lot of time convincing herself that she'd made up… Well, everything when it came to Valentino. There had been months in there, maybe even a whole year, where she'd felt she had no choice. She'd had to convince herself that she suffered from nothing at all but an overactive imagination, or die.

Because he was marrying another woman. And she had been given absolutely no choice but to live with that.

But any doubt she might have had on that score was swept away when his mouth took hers.

Completely and utterly and immediately.

Because if anything, the taste of him was far, far better than she'd allowed herself to remember. It was the way they *fit*. It was the heat, the power, the way she could feel his mouth as if it was on every part of her.

He kissed her as if they were both drowning in the same wild sea of sensation, and he wanted it that way. He kissed her as if he was daring her to let go, to drown with him, to let this thing swallow them whole.

It was that voracious.

He was that intense.

And it was funny, after all this time, to finally get

the thing she'd claimed she'd wanted all along. It was funny to push and push against the same brick wall only to have it open up like it had only been a door all along.

She felt a bit like stumbling. She felt a bit as if the way her feet gripped the floor below her was uncertain and precarious, and Carliz didn't know if she should step back and steady herself...or simply jump.

But when Valentino changed the angle of his mouth on hers, and he licked his way inside, she realized that her body had already made the decision.

Because this was *flying*.

So she twined her arms around his neck and kissed him back as if her life depended upon it. She felt as if it did.

When something in her began to shudder, low and deep, she knew that despite the things she'd told herself in that boat out on the water...she had not expected any of this to work. She had expected that she would sit there in that church, gearing herself up to make a scene but then not doing it. Because as angry and confused and heartsick she was over Valentino's marriage she might have been, she could not imagine explaining to her sister how and why she had found it necessary to ruin another woman's wedding.

So publicly.

And so, deep down, she had suspected that she would have been creeping back to her boat, hiding her face in her scarves so no one would see her tears, and then limping off to figure out what the rest of her life was supposed to look like. Now that love was dead and there was no need to worry about it any longer.

This was much better.

This was everything she had stopped hoping could happen. His mouth on hers, his hands spearing into her hair and gripping her, hard, in a way that made every single nerve in her body bloom bright with sensation.

Inside and out and everywhere else, because she knew Valentino in a way that no one else did. She had seen the way he was described in the press. Stern. Controlled. Methodical. They were usually insults, but she knew better. She knew that when it came to this, to the fire that burned only here between the two of them, he was all of those things—but in the kind of ways that made a woman's body not quite her own.

"You are a witch," he told her, harsh and thick against the line of her neck. "You have bewitched me."

"If I knew any spells," she said, tipping her head back to give him all the access he wanted, "I would have cast them long ago. I would not have waited for your wedding day."

He growled out a sound that thrilled her, pure and simple, from the tips of her ears down to the tops of her toes.

It was an animal sound, rough and glorious. He pulled back, so that the whole of her field of vision was that face of his, those stern and sensual planes and the glittering heat that made his faded blue eyes look like whole summers. He bent slightly and swung her up into his arms, then carried her over to his bed as if she was light as a feather.

And Carliz knew her own body very well. She and her sister had been raised by a strict mother and stricter governesses who had drilled into them the importance of their royal appearance, but what was meant by that was the appearance of effortlessness. Mila had gone through periods of struggling to maintain the size that she and the palace advisors had decided provided the best photographs, replete with elegance and sophistication, to suit a queen. Carliz had not struggled as hard, but then she was never going to be photographed with seventeen tons of ceremonial robes, a scepter, and the ancient crown—the wearing of which required perfect posture and an elegant form. As was clear from all the pictures of portly King Amadeo in the fifteenth century.

All of that to say that Carliz was five feet, ten inches tall and while she like to keep herself in the sort of shape that allowed for offhanded bikini wearing whenever she liked, she was not a twig.

But Valentino didn't seem to notice. He carried her as if she was tiny. As if she was a small, precious thing he could tuck in a pocket, if he wished.

It made her want to find that pocket, curl up in it, and maybe breathe for the first time in as long as she could remember.

He set her down on the edge of his bed, and then his hands were in her hair again. He tugged her head back. Then he dropped his face to her neck and he growled once more.

This time, it sounded like a warning.

"It's that scent," he muttered. "It's been driving me mad."

She wanted to say something amusing about that, but

she couldn't get her mouth to work, because he knelt down before her.

In a manner she could not call the least bit supplicant.

"I..." she began, but that dark fire in his blue gaze stopped her.

"Carliz." Her name was like a command, and her whole body shivered. "It is either time, or it isn't."

She understood what he was asking without him having to ask it. It was that stark. And there were a million things she might not understand about what was happening to her or why he'd resisted it for so long, but she knew she would die if they stopped. She thought she would actually, literally die.

So she nodded, though her heart was in her throat.

And then his hands were on her thighs, sleeking their way up the inside of her legs and making her gasp. Making everything in her body seem to twist into something molten as she started leaning back, as if he needed room.

Valentino didn't look up at her, so focused was he on what he was doing. He lifted her up, sliding his hands beneath her to grip her bottom as he hauled her closer to the edge of the bed and settled there, his face *right there*—

But then it stopped mattering.

Because he put his face between her legs and he breathed in, deep. And when he breathed out again, she could feel the rush of air against the most sensitive part of her, separated from his lips by only the faint scrap of silk that she wore.

He said something then, some kind of dark oath.

"Valentino," she began.

But all he did was growl and then set his mouth on her tender flesh, sucking on her as if that silk was nothing.

And her body simply…took over. Carliz arched up on the bed, as if pulled toward the high ceilings by some cord attached to the center of her chest. Her heels found their way into the center of his back, and she couldn't tell if she was pushing herself up or keeping herself still, but it didn't seem to matter.

Because he was eating her alive. And he was taking his own sweet time doing it.

That shuddering inside her tumbled in and around itself, and everything rushed toward the place where his mouth moved, flooding her, until he made a deep noise of approval. Then he shifted her, taking the heat of his mouth away. And all she could hear was her own panting, high-pitched and breathless.

There was a tug, then another one, harder still, but she didn't understand what was happening until his fingers gripped her bottom again and spread her open like a feast. Before licking his way into her molten heat at last.

And for a long while, maybe a lifetime, there was absolutely nothing but that.

The things he knew. The way he knew them, and how he showed her. The way he licked into her, moving his chin and his jaw so that everything was sensation. Everything was fire.

Still, she had the notion that this wasn't for her at all. That her pleasure was a simple by-product of his own need to taste her like this.

Somehow that made it all even hotter.

Carliz felt everything shift inside her as he moved,

as he *consumed* her. It was like a wave rising up, gathering steam, racing straight for her.

And there was a part of her that wanted to avoid it. There was a part of her that was on the verge of overwhelmed, and maybe she would even have pulled away, if only to see if she could control the heat of it, the intensity—

But he wouldn't allow it.

Valentino held her tighter. He licked in deeper.

He let his teeth scrape that proud little center of her, once. Then again—

And Carliz turned to ash.

It was a white-hot *implosion*. She heard someone scream, and her body took over, jerking into his mouth as if she was trying to ride him from below.

She could feel him shaking too. Because he was all around her, and she was holding him between her thighs, and it was only later that she would realize that the shaking she felt was his laughter. As if he couldn't believe the glory of this either.

There was nothing but that bliss.

Spitting on and on and on.

Carliz only spun back into flesh and bone when he pulled her up to sit on the edge of the bed again. His hands were on her shoulders, but it took her so long to focus on him and when she did, his mouth was in that straight, serious line. But his eyes were bright and dancing.

"Take heart, *Principessa*," he said in that low, growly voice. "This is only the beginning."

She could feel that in every single cell in her body.

And every single one of them was *blazing hot*. And so she smiled, as if this kind of thing happened to her every day. "Marvelous," she said, in some approximation of *blasé*. "It would be so disappointing if, after all this, it was just…boring."

But that lassitude making her hot and sleepy and silly disappeared in an instant when his gaze changed. When it got hotter. More intent.

"I promise I will do my best," he said in that deep, dangerous way of his. "I would not wish to bore you."

It was possible that she would come to regret saying something so flippant.

That was what Carliz thought as he stopped doing whatever it was he was doing—she realized, belatedly, that it was possible he'd been intending to undress, for she was sure that he'd been wearing a full suit before and now was simply in shirtsleeves and his trousers—and looked down at her in a way that she could only call…alarming.

In that it set off every single delicious alarm inside her body in a way she had never felt before.

She had the distant thought that she'd been playing with this fire all along, and hadn't realized it. As if it had been a wee little book of matches when he was more properly a wildfire.

He looked even more stern than before. That glittering thing in his gaze was even more intense. Valentino crossed his arms as he stood there before her, positioned between her sprawled-out legs. While she slumped there with her panties torn off and her dress hiked up to her waist.

And it didn't occur to Carliz to fidget, or to cover herself. Or to do anything but gaze back at him, wide-eyed, once again feeling small and precious and more beautiful than she ever had before in the whole of her life.

"Take off your dress," he told her.

It was an order. And…she liked it.

And he knew she liked it. His brows rose, waiting for a protest or a fight or even a reply. Maybe a laugh.

But her breath was coming faster, parts of her prickling into life and making themselves known. Her breasts felt heavy against her chest and her nipples were pinched of their own accord. Her skin felt too hot, and every time she breathed, it was as if she was causing her own dress to caress her. It made her want to squirm. Maybe she did, because she felt precious and debauched all at once. And she had never been this wet.

Ever.

And, in any case, it didn't occur to her to disobey him. She pulled the dress up and over her head in one movement and threw it aside, realizing when she saw that look of approval on his face that his approval was exactly what she wanted. She sat up straighter, as if she was offering her breasts to him, and he nodded.

"That too," he said.

Carliz's hands were shaking as she fumbled with the front closure of her bra. She peeled it off her breasts, sucking in a breath as that simple little bit of motion made her react as if he'd done it. She was oversensitized. She was shivering. And yet there was not one part of her that was cold.

"Beautiful," he murmured, and there was something about his approval that delighted her. It shimmered through her, making this hotter, making her feel molten and almost too bright with it to bear.

"You are a madness in me," he told her. "You have driven me to the limits of my control, *Principessa*, and this I cannot allow."

She didn't know what that meant. But the way he looked at her, the way he studied her as she sat there, fully naked before him, made that same shimmering, shivery heat wrap her up even more.

"The things you have done require retribution," he told her, which might have been scary if she hadn't seen that gleaming dark fire in his gaze. If she hadn't *felt* it, everywhere, as if he was still licking into her core. "Do you understand?"

"Yes," she said, though she didn't.

"Because if we are telling truths here tonight," he said, in that low, stirring way of his that she felt—again—like he was pressing the words into her skin with his tongue, "then we can admit, you and I, that the paparazzi should never have known a single thing about the two of us."

"It could be argued that they didn't. That they don't."

"Yet you will not make that argument." His eyes were stern too, then, and it made her heart ache. As if there was nothing she wouldn't do for this man's good opinion, and happily. Had that been what had motivated her all along? But no. There was also all this *fire*, the flames still licking at her as if they would never stop. They hadn't yet. "Because you know exactly what you did, Carliz. And so do I."

He moved to the bed and sat beside her, still fully clothed. And then, raising that demanding brow, he patted his thigh. "Come, then. You know as well as I do what you have earned." His eyes gleamed. "We'll start with a reminder of our sins."

For a long moment, she didn't understand. She stared at his thigh, harder than any rock beside her. Then at his face and intensity there, so all-consuming it made her wish she could simply crawl inside of him... Yet, whether she understood it or not, she couldn't stop shivering. And every single time she did, it made her wetter between her legs. It made her breasts feel heavier. It made oversensitized skin feel as if she was so raw that it might simply peel off in the next moment, leaving her brand-new and entirely his.

She didn't hate that idea.

"Carliz," Valentino said quietly. Intently. "Over my lap, please."

And then she did understand, and it slammed into her like its own explosion. Hot. Hard. Devastating.

"You... You want to...?"

"Three years." He bit off the words quietly, his eyes a bright flame. "How many tabloid stories do you think I was forced to suffer through in that period of time, thanks to you? Twenty? Forty?"

"I..." But she couldn't finish. She didn't even know what she might say.

And her heart was a trapped bird in her chest.

"Carliz."

It was the way he was looking at her. As if he fully expected her to obey him. But more, as if he needed her to. As if that was a part of this wild connection between them. As if this had been at the heart of it all along.

Carliz would have said that it couldn't have been. That there was no part of her that would ever want this kind of thing... But she wanted *him*. Her body was still tingling and shivering from what he'd already done to her. He had already proved that he knew her body far better than she did.

Her body had no qualms about any of this. Her bones felt made of nothing more than *want*.

And the fact that he wanted to spank her should have scared her. It should have turned her off immediately. If it did, she would not have cared about his approval. She would have extricated herself from this situation, no matter what.

But if anything, she was so excited she thought she might squirm off the side of the bed altogether.

"Do not make me ask you again," he said, and though his voice was hard and his mouth so firm, there was something else in his gaze. That pale blue fire, darkening by the moment.

Carliz understood that she would follow that fire anywhere. That she already had.

That if she believed she had seen his heart from across a crowded room—and she did—she could believe this, too. That this was what needed to happen.

That these things she wanted, without knowing why, were worth chasing.

So she took that same leap of faith once more. She let herself roll toward him. Then she carefully and delicately draped herself over his lap.

He shifted as she did, putting his leg between hers in such a way that she understood she would not be able to squirm off of him. She was dangling there, completely exposed to him, unable to hide anything—even the way she kept shivering with all that expectation and wild, whirling delight.

"Count," he ordered her.

And when his palm landed on the soft flesh of her bottom, she yelped.

It was not a *delight*. It *hurt*. She tried to roll away from him only to discover that her initial impression was correct. She couldn't.

Carliz opened her mouth to complain, bitterly, but that heavy palm was on the place where it smacked her, first holding it, then rubbing it. Just slightly, until all she could feel was the heat of his hand, and somehow, that sharp spike turned into something hotter. Something that sent a kind of molten thread shooting out into other parts of her, putting her on notice.

Making her squirm again, but not because it hurt.

"Count, please," he told her. "Because if I do, I am almost certain to lose my place. And if I lose count I will, naturally, have to start over."

Carliz, who had never been spanked in her life, counted each smack that this man doled out to her. And he had not been kidding about the numbers.

He spanked her, hard. He held her in place and this time, when a wave raced toward her, she found that it was a more of *whole tide*. And soon enough, she was letting wave after wave transform her as she counted, as he spanked her and spanked her, the heat of the blows mixing with the heat inside of her, until it was something new, something impossible and unwieldy and too large to bear.

This, she thought, *is what I wanted all along.*

The connection. The intensity. The riot inside her. The implacable *rightness* of his hand, its rhythm, its cadence—never faster or slower.

As if this had been what she'd wanted from him from the start. Steady. Inexorable. Something perfect she could never have dreamed of, could never have asked for.

So she melted into him and she let the tide take her away, and when he was done, she thought he murmured something like *good girl*, which made her shudder and moan even more. And then to her surprise, he shifted that hard thigh beneath her, smoothing a hand down over the curve of her bottom until he found his way to all of that molten heat she couldn't deny. And that rigid center of a need she couldn't even believe could exist after *a spanking*.

"Now come for me, *mia principessa*," he murmured and then he pinched her there, hard.

And everything inside of Carliz seemed to buckle. Then explode.

Wave after wave of sensation rocked through her until she was sobbing and writhing, and when he massaged her bottom it was a sharp, bright fire but made her come harder. And on and on it went, no beginning and no end, and it was impossible.

All of this was impossible.

And then, at last, he sat her up again and shrugged out of his clothes beside her.

She was dizzy, and delirious, or maybe it was simply that she was focused so intently on him it was as if they were the same person. She felt as if they were the same person, but so marvelously, magically split in two so it felt *this good* when they came together again.

When Valentino was naked, he crawled onto the bed and then hauled her up with him toward the head, laying her out beside him. She could feel everything, all at once. The soft linens at her back, even though they agitated the hot flesh of her bottom. And then him next to her, that hair-roughed chest as beautiful in its own decidedly masculine way as his face. It was too much to take in, all the beauty of that perfect male form of his. The ridged abdomen. The impossible perfection of his muscled arms. The ease and certainty in the way he rolled her beneath him and settled between her legs.

She made a soft sound, and his gaze lightened.

"You will feel every spank," he told her, as if he was offering her a gift. "And I give you permission to cry out as much as you need. As loudly as you want."

Her throat was dry. "I…"

"All you need to say is thank you, Carliz," he told her.

And so…she did.

Then, for the first time, she watched that mouth of his curve.

Deadly and beautiful and entirely hers.

And then he slammed his way inside her, and she… catapulted into another realm entirely.

Because everything was a wild flash of a sensation so intense it was something too new, too all-encompassing—

And everything was beautiful.

And it was all fused together, intertwined and tangled, until she found herself gripping onto him for dear life.

Her brain tried to pick apart the different sensations. The stinging in her bottom and that initial sharp pain inside of her that she had no time to adjust to—because he filled her, completely and utterly.

He filled her, and then he held her tight, as if getting his bearings, too.

She tried to breathe, but quickly realized that was not a priority. Not now.

Because there was too much sensation to bear, and yet she wanted all of it. There was too much sensation to handle, and yet she managed it. Somehow, she did it. She *wanted* to do it. She wanted *all* of it, all of him. She clenched a little bit, making him mutter a curse, but that made it better. She tested all that heavy heat wedged so deep inside her, and the more she did, the better it got.

Carliz took a breath, finally. And that was when he began to move.

She did the only thing she could think of to do. She clung to him. And then, when she realized he was setting a slow, deliberate pace, she matched his movements. The way she had when they'd danced in Rome.

The way she'd done, internally, when he'd spanked her.

It was all the same dance, she thought now.

And it wasn't as if any of the sensations dissipated.

But somehow, they all rolled into one. And he was at the center of it, thrusting deep inside her, pulling out, then doing it again.

And again.

And he was so *big*. She felt split in half and filled almost too much, but she liked it. Because every time she thought that surely she'd reached capacity, he found some new depth. And they moved together, so she had no choice but to figure out how to do this, how to make it better and better as she went. How to wrap her legs around him. How to hold on, and arch back, so he could drop his head and take one of those hard nipples into his hot mouth.

So he could make her cry out like he was teaching her melodies to brand-new songs.

Carliz had never felt both outside her skin and more inside it than she'd ever been in her life. Filled with him, and covered in sensation from her bottom and that molten core of hers and everywhere their bodies dragged together and then apart—

And then, suddenly—inexorably—the waves began to hit. One after the next.

But he didn't stop.

He kept going, so that each wave that hit was bigger, longer, wilder.

And still he went on, until she began to think the sounds she was making really were songs, and they were lost in the same sea together, and she would be happy to drown. Just like this.

Wrecked beyond repair, but flying high all the while.

His pace changed. His movements became jerky and

he rolled with her, holding her so tightly that it should have hurt, but it didn't. Carliz felt herself break wide open once more, and when she did, he shouted too.

Together, then, they tumbled end over end, one wave into the next.

And the only thought she had in her head was his name.

She didn't know how long she slept like that, but it must have been some while. When she woke, she was beneath the covers and Valentino was standing at that window again. Carliz felt a moment of cold fear that he would reset to their usual level. That they would start pretending the way they always did.

Instead, without turning around, he spoke. "I'm certain you must be hungry."

She sat up, swallowing hard when she realized that her throat was dry. There was a meal set out on the low table in front of his fireplace. And she was starving. But she didn't go to the food. She went to him instead, following an urge she'd had before yet had never indulged. Because she'd never been naked before when she'd had it. He'd never been there, wearing only a pair of trousers.

She wrapped herself around him, with her face pressed against one of the planes of muscle on his back. He started to say something, but she was still following that urge inside her, so she began to press kisses all along the smooth, hard expanse of his back. She got up on her tiptoes and pressed a kiss to the nape of his neck, then followed his spine all the way down.

And when he turned to her, there was a storm in those eyes of his. But Carliz dropped to her knees before him, put her hands on the waist of his trousers, and held his gaze as she pulled him free.

He was hard again. Bigger and bolder than she'd imagined, and she'd never thought that she would have the desire to do something like this. But this was Valentino. And she wanted nothing more than to taste him. To know him.

In every possible way.

When he didn't tell her to stop, she leaned forward and took him into her mouth.

And then, she played. She used her tongue. She experimented with suction. She licked the length of him, once and again, and got lost along the way.

But when she began to feel that ache rise inside her again, as if he was the one touching her when it was the opposite, he pulled her away.

"No," she began. "I want—"

"Too bad," he replied.

Though there was something like laughter in his eyes.

They didn't make it to the bed that time. He lifted her up in his arms, then slid her down the length of his body. He caught her thighs in his hands, holding her as she sank down over his length, until he filled her completely.

And started all over again.

It was a long time before she made it to that table in front of the fireplace, and ate her fill. Then let him treat her like dessert.

All night long, he taught her things about her body that she was a little bit afraid no one should know. Because now that she knew these things, how could she ever go back to who she was? Who she'd been before?

But she couldn't worry about that. She couldn't worry about anything.

It was the longest night of her life, and Carliz loved every moment.

And it was sometime after dawn that he tucked her beside him, anchored her with his heavy arm, and they both slept.

She woke some while later to find sun streaming in the windows and the room completely empty. More disconcerting, there was no evidence that anything had happened here. Even the bed she slept in was shockingly neat, to her eye. The tray of food they had feasted on over the course of hours had disappeared. Her dress and scarves and shoes were laid out on a chair. So neatly that it made something in her...uneasy.

Carliz spent a long time in the shower, aware that there were parts of her body she'd never felt before demanding her attention. She liked it.

Her backside ached, but the ache felt like a part of all the other marvelous things she had felt and done. So the more she was aware of her bottom, the more she was also aware of her own soft heat.

When she was dressed and somewhat pulled together, she held her shoes in her hand and padded out of the room into the grand old house she'd barely looked at yesterday while she'd been trying to find him. She knew Valentino had built it. It felt like an ancient castle, except the brilliance of it was that it wasn't, really. And so everything was modernized. Lights came on as she walked. The temperature was pleasant and perfect. It only *looked* old.

She knew enough from her own kingdom that accessible history was the kind of history people remembered. What they held dear. It was history that no one could touch or understand that people preferred to forget, then repeat.

Her own thoughts seem to sit heavy on her when she found her way to the ground floor, and discovered Valentino there.

Everything in her stilled.

He was standing in the great hall with his arms folded, his gaze trained on her as if he been waiting for her some while. And all she could think was that she had tasted every part of him now. That she knew how he *tasted*.

"I hope you're well rested," he said.

"Thank you," she replied. She waited, but he only gazed at her. "That's the most ridiculous thing you could possibly have said."

Something glittered in his gaze, but then it disappeared behind that opaque mask she knew too well. For she'd seen it too many times.

"I apologize for my intensity," he said.

Carliz stiffened. "I have not asked for an apology."

He inclined his head. "Yet I offer it all the same. I was perhaps more affected by the events of yesterday than I realized. I should not have taken them out on you."

"I think what happened between us was always going to happen," she said, carefully, as if she'd only just glanced down to find she was standing in a pile of broken glass. "Whether it was yesterday or some other day, it was inevitable."

"I do not believe that."

He said it so starkly. With such dreadful certainty. It made her feel…winded.

And he seemed to know it. He watched her so closely, as if he already knew every possible response she might have. "My security team found the boat you had waiting for you, and dispatched it," he said. "Another one is available for your use, should you need it. But of course, this is a tidal island, and low tide is in one hour. If you wish, you can take a vehicle to the mainland. Or walk."

She didn't understand. And it had been a long time since Carliz had felt so completely out of her depth. Maybe she never had been, not like this. She couldn't make sense of the fact that this man had made her feel so beautiful, so alive, and now she felt awkward. As if she'd misunderstood. As if she'd made this all up, all along.

"Valentino," she began.

"You and I will never see each other again," he told her, and he looked at her directly as he said it. There was nothing particularly opaque in his gaze, not then. It was direct. It was certain.

It was heartbreaking.

"I don't understand," she whispered.

"What I can tell you is what I have told you all along," he said, and she hardly recognized his voice. Too smooth. Too controlled, when he had groaned out his pleasure against the flesh of her breasts. "This is impossible. Last night should never have happened. There is no you and I, Carliz. There never will be."

Then, impossibly, he turned and walked away.

Though, to her shame, she didn't truly believe he was

leaving her there until she heard the sound of a helicopter flying off above her.

And no one was there to see her when she let her knees buckle. When she slid down to the floor. There was no one there as witness, no one to see her cry.

That was a good thing, because she was there a long time.

But eventually, the floor grew too hard, too cold. She remembered what he'd said about the tide.

So Carliz got to her feet. She gathered up her scarves and what remained of her dignity, and she walked off that damned island, determined not to look back. Not to waver. Not to make even the faintest wish that things could be different, because they weren't.

She had been a fool, plain and simple.

And when her feet touched the mainland, she vowed there and then on the whole of Italy and Europe stretching out behind it that she was done with Valentino Bonaparte.

For good.

CHAPTER FOUR

THREE MONTHS LATER, on a late September day that was blue and cool with hints of the glorious summer that she had seen here with her own eyes in July, Carliz stood on an Italian beach at low tide and hated...everything.

Mostly herself.

Well. No. Mostly one Valentino Bonaparte, but *herself* came in a close second.

"I do not want to do this," she muttered, letting the spiteful little breeze steal her words and send them tumbling down the beach toward the village that had stood right where it was since long before there were any Bonapartes kicking about.

Or any Sosegadases, for that matter.

But there was no point in her having come back here if she wasn't going to do the thing she'd come to do, so she forced herself to start walking.

She remembered walking off the island last time all too well. The shoes she'd chosen to potentially stop a wedding had proved unequal to the task, so she'd had to do it barefoot. In the previous night's dress of scarves and mystique.

If there had ever been a walk of shame more complete, Carliz really could not imagine what it might look like.

It was almost funny, she had thought that morning as she'd walked away from all things Valentino Bonaparte, her toes cold in the wet sand and every single muscle in her body screaming out in a full-throated, brand-new voice. She had been accused of many, many a walk of shame in her day. All she really had to do was appear in public before noon and some or other walk of shame was assumed and then speculated upon. Just as any indication that she'd been so much as introduced to a man meant, to all the tabloids, that she was dating him. She'd always found it all entertaining in the extreme.

Likely, she'd discovered that day, because she'd never done the things they'd accused her of doing.

Because that walk away from Valentino's personal castle had taught her that she was not meant to be like the people who did these things on the regular. No shame to any of them, of course. She envied anyone's ability to love themselves enough that it didn't matter whether or not anyone else did.

That was not how she'd felt that day. She still couldn't really imagine putting herself in a position like that again, much less with someone else. Or with someone new. The very idea made her feel ill, then and now.

Back in July she'd tried to convince herself that it was all for the best that she'd had that long walk ahead of her, with more than enough time than anyone would need to sort these things out in their head, surely.

She'd assured herself she was emotionally sorted when she'd arrived on the shores of mainland Italy and had then turned to the actual details of rescuing herself from her own folly. It was possible that she taken her time with that rescue, despite her self-assurances. She'd called her unamused security team once she'd gotten on a train to Rome so they could meet her there. She'd spent a few days in one of her favorite spas, complete with ancient baths and mandated silence, and then a rather leisurely route back home into the mountains of Las Sosegadas.

Where Mila had been waiting with a stack of international papers the palace staff curated for her perusal and entirely too many questions about the called-off wedding of the man the whole world thought she'd had that epic affair with.

I was not invited to Valentino's wedding, Carliz had replied, calmly. But it was the sort of calm that was undercut with the kind of steel she used very rarely. Which, of course, had only made her sister's brows rise higher. *Therefore, anything that occurred there has nothing to do with me.*

It's very scandalous, Mila had replied in her usual manner, though she looked more speculative than normal. She waved her hand at the collection of papers. *Everyone is speaking of it. And, of course, as his most notable ex-girlfriend, your name is coming up. Quite a lot.*

If there was a better definition of reaping what one sowed, Carliz had already slept with him. But that she'd created an affair that hadn't happened until now, and that she would very much like to pretend had not happened at all, ran a close second.

She'd made herself shrug, though nonchalance had felt difficult to come by. *You know as well as I do that no one can control what the tabloids choose to speculate about, Mila.*

Carliz had suffered through a similar interrogation from her less sedate mother, then had taken herself off to her apartments in the palace, curled up on her bed beneath blankets she did not need for warmth, and wondered what the hell she was going to do with the rest of her life.

Slowly, she came to think that the way Valentino had chosen to reject her that terrible morning had helped. Because she had always believed that if he would just give in to the chemistry between them, he would *see*. He would *know*.

He would stop telling her that it was nothing.

And it turned out that he did see. He did know—and he still wanted nothing to do with her.

In its own way, that was really very liberating.

A few days later, when she'd grown tired of acting *perfectly fine* to her family while assuming the fetal position in private, she'd found herself in the studio space she'd long kept for herself in the palace. It was an airy room in her apartments that she hadn't so much as walked into in ages. Or even thought about. But she'd once found painting a more appropriate emotional release than, say, planting stories in tabloids.

Carliz had settled in with a sense of purpose. She'd looked through all of her half-finished canvases and she'd sat down before the one she'd loved the most, certain that at any moment, inspiration would strike and she would leap into one of those painting fevers that had used to take her over in school. She would go off on an oil paint bender that would last until the painting was done and she emerged, feeling reborn and victorious, on the other side.

But no matter how long she sat there, she never touched brush to canvas.

She looked all the colors, all the shapes, and saw Valentino. She saw the things that they had done. She felt his handprint, hard and red against her bottom.

It had taken days to fade.

She had cried—hard—when it finally had.

Carliz had been home for nearly two weeks when her mother once again brought up the subject of an appropriate husband. This time, the Queen Mother chose to do it at one of their usual weekly family dinners, just the three of them. Her Majesty the Queen, the queen mother in her typical shroud, and the normally bright and shiny Princess Carliz, who was not sure that she would ever feel sparkly or at all like herself again.

Mother, Mila had said reprovingly after a lengthy monologue on the implications of both the queen and the Princess Royal's enduring single state as well as what the appearance of a tight family unit would do to bolster support for the monarchy, her favorite topics, *can you not see that Carliz is suffering? A man she was very close to had a very well-publicized breakup and yet has been notably absent from Carliz's vicinity, so one can only assume that Carliz's affections were not returned. She needs grace, not dating advice.*

It was nearly unbearable, Carliz had thought then, her

gaze on the plate before her, to have it all boiled down like that. Her sister might as well have said, *he's just not that into you.* Because it amounted to the same thing, didn't it?

She had forced herself to look up. She'd forced a smile at her sister, then had looked at her mother.

You keep going on about wanting me to marry, she'd said. *But I am quite certain that in one of the twenty thousand or so extremely boring lectures that we received as girls about our duties, responsibilities, and so on, Her Majesty the Queen herself must marry first.*

She certainly should, their mother began.

I will not be marrying for some time, Mila had said then, in that firm way that made it clear she was speaking as the queen, not as a family member. Even their mother inclined her head. Mila toyed with her wineglass. *Our father regrettably died too soon. I am too young, I think. I will need to wait some while before I can be certain that whoever marries me does not harbor any aspirations to power.*

Understandable, murmured their mother with great sympathy, because her reverence for the crown and its pronouncements knew no ceiling. Only days before she had been ranting to Carliz that Mila *must* marry, and soon, to secure her legacy.

Very well then, Carliz had said, to her own surprise, perhaps because she was tired of gazing despondently at her plate. *I suppose I might as well carry on the family legacy until Mila is ready.*

When no one had responded—an excessively unlikely occurrence with her family—she had looked up again to find the pair of them staring back at her with differing levels of shock. Mila's was tinged with curiosity, her mother's with suspicion.

I'm not joking, Carliz had clarified. *I need to do something with my life. As Mother has pointed out repeatedly, and more vocally by the day, it might as well be doing my duty to crown and country.*

And really, it hadn't been that bad. She had heard her friends from school speak of far more painful dating scenarios that they underwent simply because they were seeking a partner in life, and they didn't have an entire palace team involved to act as a buffer.

First there had been a great many meetings with the team assigned to the mission of getting the Princess Royal married. They had started off with a startlingly thorough dig through her entire life, asking all manner of impertinent questions.

I would hope, Carliz had said at one point, her manners beginning to fail her, *that the fact that I am a royal princess, sister to the queen of Las Sosegadas herself, should stand in place of whatever curriculum vitae it is you're building here.*

Indeed, huffed her mother, who had been sitting in.

Rather shockingly, Carliz had thought. It was so... supportive.

Forgive me, Your Highness, the chief aide in charge of the marriage operation had said at once. *This is not a CV, for, naturally, you do not need to sell yourself. You are the prize. We are only gathering as much information as we can to help us choose the appropriate partner for you to consider.* There had been the slightest, deferential pause. *And, of course, only those who complement not only* your *strengths, but the kingdom itself.*

Carliz did not mention a stern mouth and pale blue eyes. She had not allowed herself to think of such things in the light of day—though her dreams did as they pleased—and anyway, it had been clear that only she thought they complemented each other at all.

She had heard a lot about the needs of the kingdom after that. As if her family wasn't intimately and intricately linked with the kingdom in too many ways to count. As if she, herself, had not spent the whole of her life in the kingdom and of the kingdom, and therefore could not possibly understand it.

But the good news, she'd thought as she sat in all those meetings and resolutely refused to think of Valentino no matter how many potential suitors they paraded before her, was that she was *fine* as time went on.

Perfectly fine.

True, she'd felt a little gray around the edges. Some people might call that a touch of depression, but that wasn't something members of her family were permitted to suffer from, so she certainly hadn't claimed it as such. And besides, she'd had nothing at all to be depressed about. Her days had been filled with worthy appointments. In service to the queen, she'd cut ribbons to open things and had made grateful little speeches of commendation that she'd forgotten entirely the moment the words were out of her mouth. She'd smiled, she'd posed, and she'd no longer bothered to argue with the soulless wardrobe department in the palace, who were forever trying to dress her as if it were still the 1940s and there was a war on.

Carliz had assumed that the strict policy she'd taken of no longer allowing herself to dwell on anything involving Valentino Bonaparte—not her memories, not any stray mention of him in the papers, as if the man did not exist—was the reason that she often felt...unwell. Not actually *sick*. She'd just had a general sense of ongoing malaise that she'd assumed would pass.

Eventually.

Because all things passed *eventually*.

Or maybe it wouldn't, she'd found herself thinking sometime in the beginning of September. But so what? It was probably better for everyone involved, from her sister on down to the subjects who clapped so wildly when they saw her in the street, that Carliz pretend she'd never known what it was to sparkle in the first place.

Because, after all, that had always been an act.

Maybe that was the part that needed to pass, she'd thought. Maybe this was the new, improved, *mature* version of her. As September had started, the team had begun to send her out on carefully curated dates. Though, functionally, they were more like interviews. The men had already been briefed that they were being considered as potential husbands for the famous Princess Carliz. Accordingly, they were all perfectly polite. They were all blandly good-looking in the same sort of way. They all looked...*European*, she'd supposed. They all visited exquisite tailors, which they demonstrated in their sartorial choices, suggesting a certain fashion threshold was on the palace's list. They were all happy to talk at length about their pedigrees and their portfolios, while she sat and made note of which ones had receding hairlines to match their receding chins.

The better the bloodline, the more unfortunate the chin, she'd discovered.

It sounds hideous, Mila had said one evening. She'd come home from an event and Carliz had picked up the habit of their youth, slinking into her dressing chamber when she arrived home each evening so she could lounge about while Mila got ready for bed. Because it was one of the few times she was really just...Mila.

Assuming she was ever *just Mila* any longer.

Hideous is far too strong a word, Carliz had replied, curled up on the nearest chaise with a glass of wine, though she'd found she was enjoying her wine a good deal less these days than she had once. *They are all... Perfectly nice. Eminently suitable. Astonishingly adequate, I would say.*

Her sister had shaken her head. *Damned with faint praise.*

I did not think I was praising them at all, Carliz had replied, laughing. But then had sobered when her sister had trained a very steady look on her.

I understand that it is very unlikely that I will ever meet anyone, Mila had said, but very matter-of-factly. There was no hint of self-pity in her voice. *I've come to terms with that. But I really did hope that you, at least, could have that pleasure. I thought you might even fall in love.*

I love the idea of love, Carliz had said, carefully, after a moment. She thought of her half-finished canvases.

She thought of a long, lonely walk on a sandbar in the sun, while the incoming tide threatened and there were hot handprints on her flesh. *I love the fantasy of it. I could read books about love, watch films about love, sing songs about love forever. But the reality is something else. And I think only fools pretend otherwise.*

Her sister had watched her a long moment, then changed the subject.

And so Carliz had gone out on her businesslike dates, debriefed with the team afterward, and had made no complaint about the men they selected. This had pleased no one, because her lack of any choices, for or against, made it impossible to winnow her suitors down to one clear winner.

Which was, the head aide was at pains to tell her, the point of the entire exercise.

I think I might just write all their names down on pieces of paper, Carliz had said on another night later in in the month, this time sitting next to Mila on the queen's favorite sofa in the small, private sitting room where she watched television programs she then pretended she'd never heard of when in public.

The better to remain mysterious, she always said.

Carliz had continued, *I'll throw them in a hat, then pick a name. Instant fiancé, problem solved, and we can all move on.*

Mila had actually turned toward her, pinning her with that look of hers. *This is really not what I want for you*, she had said quietly. And so kindly that Carliz had nearly felt the urge to cry. *I understand that you don't want to talk about this, but ever since Valen-*

tino Bonaparte's wedding failed to happen, you've been broody. Withdrawn. Words I would never use to describe you. If I didn't know better I would think you were…

Carliz had forced out a laugh. The bitter sound of it had been unforced. *Heartbroken? Yes, Mila. Yes, I am.*

And there had been something liberating in saying that out loud. She hadn't allowed herself that. She hadn't let herself think about her *heart* at all. And here, now, she felt…thick, everywhere, as if her heart had shattered into so many pieces she'd had to grow a protective barrier to keep from bleeding out.

She hadn't said that, though. Not out loud. *I think that everyone deserves a devastating heartbreak at least once in their life. Because that's how you discover what's important. That it's not feelings that matter, but facts. And sometimes you have to learn that the hard way.*

I wasn't going to say heartbroken, Mila said quietly, her gaze still far too kind. *I was going to say pregnant.*

Out on that very same sandbar that served as the only path to Valentino's island, and only when the tide was low, Carliz stomped on.

She had obviously dismissed her sister with a roll of her eyes. But later that night, she had found herself lying wide awake, staring at the ceiling. Because not once in that entire wicked night with Valentino had either one of them even mentioned the issue of protection.

She knew why she hadn't. *She* didn't know any better.

Or at least, she did know, but she'd never been in a position like that before, where the things that she knew completely deserted her because he'd kissed her, and he'd picked her up, and then nothing was ever the same.

But that did not excuse *him*.

She'd fretted about that for days. She'd told the team that she was deep in contemplation about her next steps regarding the husband hunt. Then she'd taken herself off to one of her favorite cities, New York, where it was easier than it should have been to sneak away from her security detail, pop into a chemist's on the nearest corner, and then slip into a bathroom in the first dive bar she came to.

Carliz had taken the test there and then.

And she had nearly caused an international incident because she'd sat in that stall so long, staring at the answer she didn't want. It had been right there before her in two little lines.

Unmistakable lines.

She had stayed in an apartment down in the West Village that she normally used as a hub while she flitted about, in and out of art museums, having lunches and dinners and drinks out with any of her millions of friends who didn't know her at all.

But this trip, she just…sat there. She ordered in food from her favorite restaurants, then didn't eat it. She stared at the walls, but what she saw was that night.

Again and again, that night.

Then, worse, the morning after.

She stayed there for almost ten days, because Carliz had absolutely no idea what she was going to do next.

And now here she was.

She had considered, at length, not telling Valentino

about her pregnancy at all. He certainly didn't deserve
to know. Every interaction they'd had had been terrible, up to and including that night and its aftermath. In
truth, the past couple of months had taught her that she
should be embarrassed that she had spent so much time
and energy chasing around after him. She was. Truly.

But the conclusion she'd come to, despite herself, was
that while all of that was perfectly valid and she could
feel about it precisely as she liked, one thing remained
true. It was not and would not be the fault of the baby.

Her baby.

Because Carliz, unlike Valentino, was not made of
stone and spite, she was also capable of feeling empa-
thetic about the things she knew about his history. About
the father who had carried on with the housekeeper in
the house where he'd lived with his wife. So that both
wife and housekeeper were pregnant by him at the same
time—though the news about their sons' true relationship was not disclosed until later.

Carliz knew that she was many things, not all of them
flattering or fabulous in the least, but she'd like to think
she was not cruel. If Valentino wished to treat his child
the way his father had treated him, that would have to
be his choice to make. She would not do that choosing
for him.

She had interrogated herself on this topic all the way
to Italy. Was she truly acting out of that sense of what
was right? Or was she using this as an excuse to see
Valentino again?

But every time she asked herself that, she thought
about those final moments with him in the hall. That

opaque mask he'd worn, after everything they'd done with each other all through the night.

And her stomach never failed to turn.

It did again now.

"No," she muttered. "This is not about seeing him."

She'd had the palace physician snuck in to see her when she returned home from New York. The doctor had confirmed what she already knew, that she was nearly three months along. But better yet, the baby was thriving. All was well.

You look better than I've seen you in a while, Mila had said that night at dinner.

Filled with purpose, Carliz had replied, with a smile. *At last*.

And that was true in its way. Or if she did not have *purpose*, at least she had a plan.

First she would tell Valentino. When he responded negatively, as expected, she would start to plot out the next part of her life. She had decided that she needed two possible paths forward. One, a quiet life somewhere else, where she would not embarrass her sister. She rather fancied New Zealand and a magical little town on the South Island that she had visited once, Wanaka, where all kinds of creative people lived. She could simply be a single mother with the rest of them out there in the world, she thought, and raise her child in peace.

On the other hand, if Mila was inclined toward acceptance, she would have to plan her next moves with the palace.

But Valentino was the first step.

She walked and walked, keeping ahead of the tide.

And the closer she got to the island, and Valentino's house that she could see rising there on its hill, the more aware she became of her body.

Carliz told herself it was because she hadn't exercised as much as she usually did, in these last, grayish months, but she knew that wasn't quite true.

It was as if walking back across the sandbar reignited that awareness of herself that he had taught her that night. That stunning, wondrous understanding of who she really was, and what her body was truly made for, and all the astonishing things two people could do with each other.

"Including make another human," she snapped at herself, in case she was tempted to forget.

But that didn't make her breasts feel any less heavy, though not in the way they'd been heavy for the past week or so. It didn't make her feel any less thick, and not simply because her clothes didn't fit the way they'd used to.

Her body clearly remembered this island and that night, and as far as it was concerned, it was high time to get ready for more. She could feel that telltale slickness between her legs as she moved. Even her breath was shallow, as if she was already panting out all of that passion and need.

She was disgusted with herself.

Once she made it onto the island, she found herself marching down the avenue of cypress trees that led to Valentino's house. This time, there was no one else about. There was only her. And she had not worn scarves to disguise her identity, either. Carliz was dressed very simply, because this was a simple errand and nothing more. It did not call for *an outfit*. She wore a pair of jeans with an extremely stretchy waist. A pair of shoes far better suited to traipsing over the sand than the last. She wore a hat on her head to keep the sun off, because she remembered it burning her on the walk back, when she had already been more than red enough. And otherwise, she wore only a camisole beneath a roomy buttoned shirt.

Carliz thought she looked a bit like she was going on safari, though she doubted very much she would get the pleasure of hunting the particular big game she wanted today.

Just as she had three months before, she charged up the stairs cut into the side of the hill that led directly from the house's extensive gardens down to the chapel. Just as before, she marched directly up to the front door and swung it open.

But this time, she did not walk in to find the place deserted, all of the staff called off somewhere else.

This time, Valentino was standing there as if he was a statue she'd left behind in exactly the same position. Today he was at the base of the stairs, but his arms were still folded. His expression was still disapproving and otherwise, firmly opaque.

And God help her, she did not want to think about that stern mouth and all the things he could do with it. All the things that she'd been lying to herself for some while about. All the things that she would love for him to do to her again.

But she would deal with that shocking personal betrayal later.

"I believe I was very clear, Carliz, the last time we saw each other," Valentino said.

And she understood then that he had seen her coming from afar.

That he had planned this confrontation when he could instead have very simply...locked his door.

The betrayal got worse, though, because she could feel that shivering thing all over her. She hated it. And she hated him. Yet still there was something in her that was thrilled by the fact that he thought she had come back here for anything less than a good reason.

Because there was always going to be that part of her that wanted nothing more than to get naked with him again. And again.

And forever—but she shoved that treacherous thought aside.

"I cannot imagine that anyone could be more clear," she told him.

Despite herself, she took him in. She couldn't help herself. Her eyes moved all over him, looking for flaws, she told herself—but if so, she was disappointed. For there were none.

He did not look like a fallen angel, not Valentino. He looked like the sort of angel that would never dream of falling and more, would mete out retribution those who did.

And really, it would have been better for her all around if she had not thought that word, *retribution*, in his presence.

"I'm glad to see that you remain as unpleasant as ever," she continued when he did nothing but glare at her in all his disapproval. "I would have called you, as that seemed the decent thing to do, but it was made clear to me that even if I managed to obtain your phone number, it would be changed should I ever call it. Ditto your email. So here I am."

"I don't know why you cannot accept the truth of things," he said, but almost casually. Almost philosophically. "You are forcing me into a corner and I do not think you will like how I choose to step out of it."

"There is no need for you step anywhere," she told him, and it was a challenge to match his tone, but she did. "I have come a great distance—and across a vanishing sandbar, no less—to tell you something I would have much preferred to share from afar. Do you understand what I'm saying to you? I don't want to have this conversation."

"And yet here we stand."

Carliz sighed, though she would have to deal with the wound that left behind later. "After the appalling way you behaved the last time I was here, I have no wish to ever lay eyes on you again. You should congratulate yourself, Valentino. You have finally succeeded. I am entirely indifferent to you, whether you live or die, or anything else that might possibly concern you."

His brow lifted once again. Maybe as if something she'd said had landed like a weapon. Not that she should care about that.

"Carliz," he began, in a voice made entirely of warnings that her body took as dark, delicious promises—

something else she would need to unpack later, when she was alone.

Later, when she knew she'd survived this.

She lifted a hand to stop him. "I'm having your baby," she said. Direct and to the point, and it did not matter what he did with that, not now it was said. "You can do with that information what you will."

And then she finally—*finally*—did the right thing.

She turned on her heel and marched to the front door, leaving him of her own volition. Something she wasn't sure she was capable of doing until she did.

Then she started for home.

CHAPTER FIVE

SHE TURNED AROUND and exited the house so quickly that, at first, Valentino was tempted to imagine that this was yet another one of his far too realistic fantasies where the troublesome Princess Carliz was concerned. He'd been plagued by them since the night of his doomed wedding. They'd so far showed no sign of abating.

Surely this was yet another indication that the woman was still haunting him—that he needed to work harder to exorcise the demon in him that was this infernal need for her. This impossible *wanting*.

He stood there as if he was a part of the statuary that lined the hall, but the way his heart was beating—much too fast and much too hard—told him otherwise. Despite his best efforts, he was not made of marble. He was all too regrettably human. And that likely meant he had not made her up.

Much less what she had come to tell him.

Before he could form a thought, much less a plan based on reason rather than the chaos of desire, he was following her.

He threw open the door she'd slammed shut behind her and was surprised to see that she was moving at a fast clip through the garden, when he would have said that Carliz was not the sort to hit such speed. He had never seen her do anything but *glide*. And she was not *running*, exactly, but she was clearly doing her best to get away from him as fast as she could.

It was an unnerving sensation to see her moving away from him.

Valentino could not say that he liked it. At all.

Grimly, he set off after her. He had told himself—repeatedly—that he would not keep tabs on her, but he had failed in that. Almost immediately. He had found himself scouring the papers both on and offline, telling himself he was only looking to see what had become of his reputation in the wake of the wedding scandal his brother had forced upon him. Handily enough, every article or segment on the subject mentioned Carliz too. He'd steeled himself to see her out on the party circuit once again, selling her take on the scandal to the paparazzi so they could torture him with his brother's perfidy and his fiancée's shirking of her vows, but instead it was as if Carliz had fallen off the face of the earth.

It only went to show how hard she had worked in the first place, he had been forced to conclude, to make the relationship they'd never had a topic of such interest to so many.

Valentino had never thought he would miss that.

Then again, he'd also imagined that he'd have better sense than to put his hands on that woman. The woman he'd wanted from the first moment he'd seen her, but had known at a glance was not for him.

Because he knew what happened when people gave in

to their wants at the expense of their responsibilities—
and even their souls. He'd watched it play out before
him in real time and he'd lived through the aftermath.
He was still living through the aftermath.

And now, to add to the trauma of his father's love tri-
angle and all the pain it had caused, now Carliz haunted
him too. All night, every night, and all through the day
as well.

Valentino was ruined in ways he had not imagined
possible.

He was a wreck of himself and it was all her fault,
but he knew that he was the one to blame.

The proof of that was the fact he was chasing after
her now, when he should have let her go. The way he
should have done that night in Rome. He should have
turned and walked away from her, not toward her. He
should never have taken her in his arms. They should
never have danced.

But it was too late for all of that now.

Valentino caught up to her at the base of the hill, in
front of the chapel where he had not gotten married.

He reached out, then dropped his hands before he
caught her by the elbow and steered her around to face
him. Because nothing good came from putting his hands
on Carliz.

Nothing good at all, no matter how it felt at the time.

"I beg your pardon," he said, falling into step with her
and sounding far calmer than he felt, because he knew
that was perhaps the only weapon he had in a situation
like this. Assuming there were any weapons to be had
when it seemed he'd gone and blown up his own life—

as if, after all, his father's poison was not as deeply buried in him as he'd thought if that was even possible. "I could not have heard you correctly. It sounded as if you said…?"

"That I'm having your child?" Carliz stopped walking with the same sort of force she'd used to slam his door behind her, and rocked back on her heels as if she nearly bowled herself over. She swept the wide-brimmed hat she wore off of her head and smoothed a hand over her hair, never shifting that wary, clever gaze of hers from his, its very steadiness its own affront. Or so he chose to call it, that tension inside of him. "Do you want to guess how far along I am? Go ahead. I bet you'll get it on your first go."

"Impossible," he said at once.

Except…was it?

He had spent a lot of time going over that night in minute detail. And one thing that he could not remember doing, at any point, was taking a moment to handle his own protection. He had thought of that failure later, but not in terms of any potential pregnancies. More in terms of the fact that he should not have been surprised it felt so good. As if she'd been fashioned specifically for him.

Everything feels good without a condom, he'd lectured himself scathingly. That wasn't revolutionary, it was simply a fact that men had been whining about for ages.

"Do you need me to give you a lesson on human biology?" Carliz was asking, her own voice too close to scathing for his liking, though he should have exulted in it as more evidence that she belonged far, far away from him. "It's really very simple. If you have sex and don't do anything to prevent pregnancy, lo and behold, a pregnancy can occur."

"I assumed you were on the pill," he said. Because it was the only thing he could say. It was also the truth.

But she looked back at him in the same narrow way, with no change of expression. "Why would I be on the pill?"

"You cannot possibly depend on your lovers to protect you." He detested saying that out loud, as Valentino found he did not wish to imagine her with other men. Equally, he did not wish to ask himself why that was when he had never been at all interested in the other pursuits of his partners. "Men, as I proved myself to my shame, are not equal to the task."

He didn't like saying that, either, having prided himself his whole life on being more than the equal of any task set before him. But it was true no matter if he liked it. Or didn't like it.

Carliz shook her head, still looking at him as if there was something wrong with *him*. "Is that... Are you putting on the fact you got caught up in the heat of that moment—like anyone else would and I certainly did— as another hair shirt for you to wear?"

She made a scoffing sort of sound while he tried to take that in. A hair shirt? *Another* hair shirt? He had never been quite so Catholic, surely. But he suddenly had the urge to adjust the shirt and coat he was wearing.

He repressed it.

"Spare me, Valentino," Carliz said before he could protest her characterization of him. "Please. I wasn't on the pill because I've never had any reason to be on the pill. And I didn't ask you to use protection because it quite literally never occurred to me." She let out a bitter little laugh. "Not a mistake I intend to make twice but really, once does the trick."

And he couldn't stand this. Not just what she was saying about her pregnancy or the way she was looking at him. All this time he'd been so sure that he knew her, if against his will. This woman was irrepressible. There was nothing bleak about her.

Until now.

It was like looking at his mother all over again.

Except this time, it wasn't his father who had done this thing. It was him. He had turned into his father without even realizing it.

The very idea made him feel sick.

"You are right," he managed to get out, tersely. "I should not attempt to make this a failure of responsibility on your part. We share the blame. I apologize. I will admit that I'm surprised that a woman like you made mistakes like that, but then, I'm equally surprised that I did the same."

He was pleased with that. It was equitable. They were both adults. There was no need to descend into any puerile mudslinging when they'd both been in the same bed.

But Carliz tilted her head to one side and stared at him in a way that he found...distinctly uncomfortable.

"A woman like me," she repeated, as if they no longer spoke several of the same languages. "Do you mean a virgin, Valentino? Because I was a virgin that night. You took my virginity, as a matter of fact, and quite thoroughly. You even spanked me, and I liked it. *And then* you told me that you never wanted to see me again." Her eyes were bright in a way he'd never seen before, and there was color on her cheeks that he assumed was the bloom of her temper. "I apologize if in the middle of all of that I didn't have the time or wherewithal to give you chapter and verse on my feelings about birth control and my lack of experience overall."

He only stared at her, not sure whether he wanted to let his own temper surge, or possibly just kiss her again, and both options made him loathe himself. Carliz made a noise, somewhere between frustration and disgust.

Then she stepped around him, and carried on stomping back toward the beach and the sandbar that was still visible at this point. Though the tides were always turning, wholly uninterested in the affairs of men.

There were very few moments in Valentino's life where he had felt as if the world had been picked up and shaken from end to end like a tawdry snow globe. As if at first it stopped abruptly enough to send everyone reeling, and then everything he knew was shaken away.

The first time had been when he was twelve. And had discovered that the best friend he considered a brother was, in fact, his *actual* brother.

The second was the night his mother had died, and the understanding he hadn't wanted that night—that his father could have saved her, or at least tried to save her, but he had not. He had *chosen* to wait for the tide to go down.

This was the third.

Because if his princess had been a virgin that night,

and he could not imagine why she would lie about something like that, then everything he thought he'd known about her was wrong. Or off-center, somehow.

He, who had always prided himself was wrong. Horribly, shockingly wrong.

Again, something in him whispered, like a terrible smoke winding deep inside him. The way he had been about his family and his whole damned life as a child. The way he had been about his father, who he had never liked much, but had not understood was an actual monster until that night.

He didn't know how long he stood there, but then, once again, he had to chase her down the lane in an effort to catch up.

"Let me guess," she said, her cheeks flushed with more of that hot temper he hadn't known she had, as she charged toward the beach, "now you're going to tell me that you don't believe me. You will demand that I somehow prove that I was a virgin then, when it is obviously much too late. When you know perfectly well that pain was part of the pleasure that night, because you taught me that."

"Carliz."

And he didn't mean to use that voice. He didn't think he meant it, but it was the one that she'd obeyed without thinking that night. She did again, now. She stopped dead.

And when she looked at him, there was a wariness in her gaze.

"I believe you," he told her, in a low voice that was

not *that* voice, but was raw all the same. "And I did not mean to hurt you."

Something crackled through her, like that electricity that was so much a part of her spilling over. But this time, it was fused with that flushed hot temper of hers, too.

"I didn't say you hurt me," she belted out at him. "*I* wasn't hurt. *I* wasn't the one who woke up that morning and decided to be awful, pretending once again that there was nothing between us. I don't know what this is right now either." She threw out a hand toward him, and he didn't know if she meant to point at him or it was simply a decorative gesture. "Suddenly you're understanding? Suddenly you have some deep interest in my well-being that you've never shown before now? Let me guess. You're already calculating how you can use my pregnancy to your advantage. You're already wondering how you can spin it so that you once again come out on top of your brother. Whatever that looks like this month."

He hadn't been thinking that. But he couldn't deny that it was entirely likely that he would have started at any moment. Had he not been so shocked by her announcement, he likely would have convened his press people already to get them working on the appropriate stories to seed.

Still, Valentino didn't like the fact that she'd called him out on that. He didn't like it at all.

"What exactly was your plan?" he demanded. "You thought you would drop in, drop a small bomb and then…what?"

"I have a great many opportunities available to me, as a matter of fact," she told him with a certain loftiness that he assumed royals were taught at birth. "Thank you so much for asking. I spent most of the last three months looking for an appropriate husband." He must have made some kind of face at that, when he prided himself on being unreadable under all circumstances. But she laughed. "I'm sorry. Is that upsetting to you? Are you the only person alive who gets to go out and find someone to marry because they fit a checklist?"

His jaw was so tight that he was afraid he might snap a tooth, but he couldn't seem to unclench it enough to respond. She made that noise again.

Then she turned once more, and kept going.

Valentino had to stay where he was for a moment, breathing a little more heavily than was wise, because while he did not want to think about her other lovers, he *really* did not like the idea of her married to someone else.

He found that he hated it.

But he told himself that was perfectly valid. After all, she was carrying his child.

This time when he drew up beside her she had made it to the small path that led down from the lane to the beach.

"Obviously any marriage plans you might have will have to be put on hold," he told her, possibly with a touch more severity than was called for. "I do not intend to share custody of my child, Carliz. You should know that at once."

"You've known about this child for exactly fourteen

minutes," she threw back at him without even looking over his way. Then she did, even shoving that hat backward on her head to really make sure he saw the seriousness all over her face. "I will not be putting anything on hold for you. Ever again. Of that, you can be one hundred percent sure, Valentino."

"Then why did you bother to come here?" He moved closer to her than was necessary, and much closer than was wise. "Why would you tell me that you are carrying my child, the heir to my family legacy, if you intend to marry another?"

Carliz made a slight, instantly repressed movement, and he had the mad notion that what she really wanted to do was put her hands on him. He wanted that too. Badly.

Because if she put her hands on him, he knew exactly what would happen next, and he didn't care if his brother, his former fiancée—his sister-in-law, he reminded himself—his awful father, and the whole of the Italian mainland lined up to watch them.

Maybe some of that showed on his face too, because she wisely kept her hands to herself.

"You act as if I've done something to you, Valentino." The wind caught at her hair and he could see the pert impression of her nipples behind her shirt, though he knew it was not the temperature that was pinching them to attention like that. Or not only the temperature. Because the chemistry between them, as ever, was nearly all-consuming. "You act as if this is all my fault."

She blew out a breath, but before he could counter that he had not even once suggested that she'd tried to trick him, or that she was foisting another man's child on him, or even questioned her too closely on the matter—as he had heard in places like the Diamond Club that many of his peers had done from time to time—she kept on.

"Something happened between us in Rome that changed everything," she said, as if saying it was forbidden but she was doing it anyway. Her eyes got big, trained on him the way they were while the fall sunshine spilled down over her shoulders like it was as attracted to her as he was. "I'm sorry that you're too terrified of that reality to even have a conversation about it. But I'm not an idiot. I'm fully aware that neither one of us walked into that event planning for anything like *that* to happen. At any point over the past few years, you could have had an honest conversation with me about the fact that it did, but you never have. I regret how I acted in the course of those years, but I did it because I truly believed that there was something there worth fighting for. I have no idea what you were doing."

Valentino wished he couldn't hear the way her voice scratched at that. He wished he couldn't remember those years himself.

"And no," she said, raising her voice when he started to say something—though he wasn't sure if he meant to defend himself or possibly just apologize, "I don't want to hear what you have to say about it now. It exploded the night of your wedding the way it was always going to, sooner or later. There's no going back from that. But now I'm carrying a child."

She reached down to put her hand on her belly, and he had been too busy drinking in the sight of her. The fact of her, not the shape of her. The brightness all around her. The way light seemed to find her wherever she went, sunlight or lamplight alike. The way her eyes gleamed and her cheeks flushed.

Then, too, he'd been remembering the way she squirmed as she lay over his lap, sobbing first in pain and surprise, then with the pleasure of it.

But now that she put her hand on her belly, he could see that her shape had changed. That she had a notable roundness there, when before her stomach had been slightly concave. Something he would know, because he had spent a great deal of time tasting every inch of the span between her hipbones that night before moving lower.

"I never really thought about having children," she told him, still holding her belly and his gaze with the same sort of steel. "It was something I assumed I would do, somewhere down the road, because everyone does. My mother has always been going on at me about doing my duty to the family and producing potential heirs, particularly since my sister seems dead set on reigning as the Virgin Queen of our time. Someone will have to succeed her and if it is not me, or one of my children, it will all have to go to a cousin who none of us can stand. So you see the dilemma."

"I don't."

She scowled at him. "I was going to have to have a child anyway. And I have accepted the fact that it will happen now, not later. I did not intend to have *your* child, Valentino. And that is really all I came here to tell you. The child exists. I expect nothing from you. And you can continue to play these games of denial and blame that you've been engaged in from the start, but I don't want to be involved in them anymore."

Carliz turned around again on that note, but this time with great dignity, as if she thought that might shame him. And maybe it could. Maybe it would.

But not right now.

She set off across the beach, but the tide was already coming in. Still, she was moving at a fast enough pace that if she kept it up, she should only get a little bit wet on the other side. There would likely be no compulsory swimming to make it to shore.

He watched her leave him again.

He didn't like it any better.

And once again, Valentino's heart was heaving about behind his ribs as if he'd run a marathon or two today. These had been a strange few months. There had been the fact that his brother had stolen his bride and married her, right under his nose, that he kept waiting to hit him like the betrayal it was. But he knew it wasn't going to. He was furious that his brother had spoiled his plans, that was all. He didn't really care that Aristide and Francesca were married. He only cared that they'd embarrassed him.

He only cared that he'd had to hear his father's taunts and jeers on that topic, when he had dutifully stopped by for a dinner he'd put off as long as possible. He subjected himself to one per season, so little could he tolerate anything that Milo said or did.

This time, it had been even worse than usual, but not because Milo was getting any hits in with his snide remarks about what Aristide and his *worthy* little heiress wife must be up to. But because he had been thinking of the wedding night he'd had despite misplacing his intended bride. And because that night with Carliz had left him too raw. As if she'd flayed some essential armor away from his skin without him realizing it and he didn't know how to go about replacing it.

He told himself it was irritating, nothing more.

But the truth was that he had spent far too much time remembering all the details of that night over the course of these last three months. And all the ways that she had proven herself to be absolutely perfect for him in every way.

Sexually compatible, he liked to correct himself. That was all he meant by that.

Because a truth he had come to accept a long time ago was that he had certain needs and preferences. And it was a fact that mostly, he could not allow them to be met in any satisfying manner. He had vowed that he would be the respectable Bonaparte. That he would live up to his mother's ideals of who he could be, though she had fallen far short herself. And he had held his grandfather's example of dignity and moderation above all else.

None of that went hand in hand with the kind of sex he liked best.

Valentino also knew that a great many men on this earth had allowed themselves to be brought low because they were controlled by their sexual urges. He did not intend to become one of them—though her comment about hair shirts just now cut deep, because that was precisely how he'd thought about his marriage.

He and Francesca had never had any chemistry,

though he thought she might have attempted to manufacture some, at the start, because it was expected. But he had not wanted that from her. It had been easy to tell at a glance that she was not the kind of woman who would find the games he liked to play at all entertaining.

Valentino had assumed that he was done with them. That he would sacrifice those things on the altar when he made his vows. He had been planning to get married that day not knowing if he and Francesca would even have a sex life. There were other ways to have heirs, after all. At best he had expected something dutiful and rare, and otherwise had expected they would go about their lives as they pleased.

Then the princess had appeared the way she always did. The Carliz storm, sweeping into his bedroom, and making a mockery of every vow he'd ever made to himself.

And then to discover that on top of all the other ways that she had ruined him already, it turned out that she was the kind of very special, very unusual woman who could meet every need he had…

She had wrecked him.

Again and again.

He had woken so early that morning that he wondered if he'd slept at all. He had felt not simply replete, the way anyone could after a release such as that. He'd felt something else. Something he wanted to call *recharged*, though it had felt something far more than merely physical.

Valentino had not wanted to accept that feeling at all.

He had rolled out of bed, telling himself that he absolutely would not look back at her, but then he did.

Breaking one more vow where she was concerned—and that had been the part that had pricked at him. To him, Carliz was nothing more than an addiction. That was her role in his life. He'd had one taste and she might as well have been heroin.

The way he had *hungered* for her.

When he'd looked back, he could muster up his own outrage. Because she'd looked more beautiful every time he looked at her. And never more so than on that morning, curled up in his bed with smudges of exhaustion beneath her eyes as she slept—because she had met him no matter what he'd thrown at her. She had exceeded expectations he hadn't even known he'd had.

He was very much afraid that she had ruined him for all other women.

That was unacceptable.

He had left his rooms, like a ghost. And he had built this place himself, a monument to the family he'd never had and the legacy he'd hoped to build, though his brother had always called it a mausoleum.

So perhaps it was not a surprise that he found himself in the gallery he kept because all great houses had galleries, featuring portraits of his family. Never his father. But his mother sat there, looking regal and lovely, whole and almost happy. And the next portrait, his grandfather stood behind a chair where his grandmother was perched, the two of them smiling just slightly. As if they did not wish to get too overwrought in the presence of the artist.

And he had seen where passion led. He had watched

it play out in real time, to desperate and terrible ends. If there was one promise that he could keep in his time on this earth, it would have to be that one that he'd made when the truth about his family had come out.

He would never, ever allow himself to become a slave to passion.

Valentino had watched it rip his mother apart. Because she had loved his father despite everything. And it had not made even one bit of difference.

His father, for his part, had only shrugged, or laughed, and asked what a man could be expected to do? *Passion always wins in the end*, Milo had told them all.

Valentino had sworn it off then and there.

So that was what he did when he next saw her. He had sworn Carliz off, because it was the right thing to do.

But now she was walking determinedly out of his life, while carrying his baby.

And he was forced to recall that there had always been one thing that he'd held far above passion. His duty.

And his family legacy, whether he cared for his current family or not.

He caught up with her one final time, standing there on a sandbar while the sea closed in on two sides.

This time, she only glared at him.

"We will fly to London," he told her. "I wish to have my doctors there run every test there is, to make sure that both you and the child are well."

"Because, obviously, I have failed to do that myself."

"You're not the only one who requires peace of mind, Carliz," he bit out.

But she studied him. "And you'd also like a little blood test, I imagine. Just be sure."

He neither confirmed nor denied that. "Either way, there is no need for you to hike back to the mainland. We'll be leaving shortly."

"To what end?" Carliz demanded, and she really did yell that out then. To the sea. To the sky. To Italy in the distance, where it had sat for millennia. Where they would be nothing but a wisp of memory, one day, like everything else. Valentino did not find that thought as comforting as he usually did. He did not like the thought of Carliz disappearing. Even while she continued to yell at him. "No matter what you discover with that testing won't admit you're going to do, what does it matter? I've already told you—"

"I will need to confirm that the child is mine," he told her, as dispassionately as he could. "Not because I question you, but because my legal team will, and so will anyone else who tries to contest my will and testament." He expected her to argue that, but she didn't. Because, of course, she was a royal. She knew all about contested wills and the importance of a documented trail of bloodlines. "Once I do, Carliz, we will be married."

CHAPTER SIX

THE COLD RAIN in London was a shock after the island with all that bright, golden light, the sound of seabirds wheeling about overhead, and the sea itself, there in the corner of every glance, every look.

Carliz found a certain comfort in it, however. She had always loved London. She'd spent a great deal of time here, over the years, and there was something about the muted colors and the layers of gray on gray. There was something about the bright pops of color, here and there, and the busy rush and tumble of an ancient city in modern times.

Not to mention, the bleakness suited her mood.

She had not expected Valentino to react this way. It wasn't that she hadn't hoped that he might—she had, she could admit, if only in the darkest part of the night when she couldn't hide even from herself—but she'd thought that hope was foolish. In the light of day, she'd been certain she was kidding herself.

And now she felt strung out between those two extremes. What she'd braced herself for when she saw him versus that tiny little spark of hope she had tried her very best to extinguish. While the truth of things seemed strung out in the middle with her, since it didn't seem as if she was really getting either one. Whatever this was, it seemed to be some sort of…uneasy compromise and she'd spent the entire flight from the island brooding about it.

She had the time and space to brood on forever, as it happened, because it certainly wasn't as if Valentino spent any time talking to her. He had shown her to her seat, then removed himself to a different compartment of the plane, where he had conducted a number of extremely terse calls. She had been able to hear the sound of his voice in three languages, but not the words.

Maybe that was just as well. Carliz had stared out the window vaguely wishing that she might find herself a parachute and leap out when she saw the mountains, even though they weren't the right mountains. They weren't *her* mountains.

It was silly to yearn for home, but she had far bigger problems than a little bit of loneliness. Like that infernal little bloom of hope that she felt was deeply unworthy of her. It was sheer foolishness to let herself believe, even for a moment, that this man who had treated her so shabbily might somehow, magically, have gotten over that in the interim.

Right when she appeared to tell him she was pregnant, imagine that.

She already knew that he was happy to marry for convenience—why not for a child? It had nothing to do with her.

But still, there was that tiny hint of spring, down there in all that gray she'd been lost in since July. Even if it seemed to her a cruel trick of fate that all the time she tried to convince herself that she was getting over him, that she was moving on with her life, fate had been making sure she couldn't.

It didn't help that she knew too well that there had been that part of her that wanted to go back to the island all along. That had wanted to see him, once again, just to make sure that nothing had changed.

You mean, to see if something had *changed*, a voice inside challenged her. *Despite everything.*

Now, as she sat in the back seat of a sleek car that cut through the London traffic like a knife, she felt awash in too many competing emotions to count. While he sat beside her, typing on his phone and rolling calls as if he didn't have a care in the world.

In her next life, Carliz thought, she would very much like to come back as a man who could compartmentalize so many things he might as well be a stack of tiny boxes masquerading as a person.

Eventually, the car stopped and Valentino led her into a listed house in a nosebleedingly expensive part of Central London, and that was saying something when one was a literal princess who had grown up in an actual palace. The house had its own entrance round the back, past a mews house that her security was dispatched into by a simple nod of Valentino's head.

Carliz made as if to follow them, but was stopped short when Valentino merely lifted that brow of his.

She felt…chagrined, at once. Because her body reacted the way it had that night, long ago now. As if his command over her was absolute—but worse than that, as if she *wanted* it that way. Immediately, she could feel that telltale slickness between her legs. It made her want to wail out in a deep kind of grief that she refused to entertain. Not now.

Wailing would be too dramatic for a rainy afternoon. Instead, she simply followed him. As if her body was in control again, when it had already gotten her into a mess of vast proportions. Really, it shouldn't have a say.

He let her in the back door of a very old house that was small compared to his stark little fortress on the island, but impressive all the same in London. Inside, there were beamed ceilings, uneven floors, and a sense of history with every step. The building itself was so old that it somehow made perfect sense that he had furnished it so minimally, so that the history itself was the centerpiece. It had a slightly richer feel than the more popular Scandinavian and midcentury American look that was all the rage everywhere, and felt cozier for it.

Carliz decided that she hated the fact that she liked *both* of this man's homes. She would have fared much better with him if he'd brought her to some hideous corporate flat, all chrome, flash appliances, and the ubiquitous *fitness center*.

"You must have an excellent interior designer," she said as she followed him through the built-out kitchen, all greenhousey and skylit. Perhaps, she could admit as she heard the words hang in the air, a bit accusatorily.

She expected his staff to come bustling in, but no one appeared. Instead he stalked before her into his surprisingly bright and airy kitchen, where he began moving around as if this really was his own space. As if no one was around to cater to him at all.

These insights should not have curled in her the way they did, like a soft heat all its own.

"I have never consulted an interior designer," he said over his shoulder. He turned to look back at her, all arrogance. "I'm not particularly interested in the opinions of others."

"How foolish of me not to intuit that from your whole…" She eyed him, and chose not to finish the sentence. "My mistake."

"It is not that I think others should not have opinions," he said, and she felt the touch of that faded blue gaze. As intense on hers that it felt like a physical caress. Her body reacted as if it was. "But I rarely let them affect me."

She felt chastised, and that did not sit well. She turned away from him, crossing her arms over her bump, the brightness and unexpectedly welcoming feel of this house of his suddenly grating on her. "I thought you would be marching me into some kind of clinic. The better to poke and prod me so that other people can tell you things I already know. And I think you know, too."

"Carliz."

She hated the way he said her name like that. And hated far more that her body could not resist it. Could not resist *him*. Even now, when she knew what would happen. When she had lived through the ecstasy of that night—and the three bitter months that had followed.

Yet she found herself turning back to him anyway. Despite her ferocious desire to do the opposite. She wanted, desperately, to walk off. To leave him here, surrounded by stark walls and cozy beams. To show him that he had no power over her.

But that would be a lie.

Valentino was watching her with a certain glittering intensity from the other side of the kitchen, the long, central counter block between them. His gaze searched hers for a moment. A breath.

Carliz felt vulnerable in a way she did not like at all.

"I have always done my very best to do my duty," he told her then, as if he'd come to some kind of heavy conclusion, and it was a dizzying thing to have what she'd thought she'd wanted all this time—Valentino finally *talking to her*—only to find she didn't want it after all. Or not like this. Not when the light outside was nothing but a bright gray and in here she was feeling more raw by the moment. "Sometimes what is dutiful comes down to the details. It can be a tedious matter of crossing *T*s, dotting *I*s, and documenting it all, but that does not make it any less of a necessary duty."

She blinked at that, not sure why it made her feel hollow inside. And after a moment, when it was clear she wasn't going to respond, he turned his attention back to the mail that had been left on his counter. Stacked neatly in a way that suggested there was some staff, somewhere. If not the butler, housekeeper, and many housemaids scenario he used on the island.

But the longer the silence stretched out between them, the more Carliz wondered if that had been... Not an apology. Not precisely. But an explanation, perhaps, which she supposed might be the same thing to a man like Valentino.

It was as if he was telling her that it wasn't that he thought she was lying. But that he had to be sure all the same.

Or maybe, came that tart voice within, *you are desperate to believe anything good about the man. No matter what he does.*

She didn't realize she let out a sound, some sort of sigh, until she found him looking at her yet again. And everything was raw. The sky above them, through the glass, was the same sort of gray that had been pressing into her for months now.

His baby was inside her. And now he knew.

Nothing was ever going to be the same. Everything had already changed, and they only had six months left to play catch-up before the *real* change came. Had she truly grasped that when she'd set out for the island this morning? Because right here, standing in a lovingly restored and cleverly remodeled kitchen in Central London, a world away from the palace in Las Sosegadas or his own island castle, she couldn't believe she'd been so determined to hurry that change along.

"Carliz," he said again, though his tone was different this time, as if he felt the rawness as much as she did. "I—"

And though her heart pattered about foolishly, almost too foolishly to bear, he never finished.

Because there was a knock on the door and then it opened almost immediately. And as a small crowd marched inside, it took her moment to get her bearings. Again.

By the time she did, she had been escorted into a small reception room and ushered into a seat while various medical personnel buzzed all around her. There were tests, a small interrogation dressed up like a medical exam, and within an hour there was no more doubt. *I*s were dotted and *T*s were crossed.

Carliz was now *officially* having Valentino Bonaparte's baby.

"I have my people working on this," Valentino told her, his voice grave.

She couldn't read him at all. Everyone had left again and it was just the two of them, sitting across from each other in a very old room with entirely too much information between them. *This* could mean anything. There were the years they'd played games around the truth of what had happened in Rome, a lightning bolt out of the blue that had never made sense, but was real all the same. There was the memory of the night they'd shared. And there was now the proof—to his satisfaction, apparently— that they had made a child out of all of that.

"Which part of *this* do you mean?" she asked, as if she had mistaken this for a charming garden party of some sort.

He stood and it made her heart hurt, then, that he was dressed so formally. That he had been dressed like that earlier. When he could not have known that she would descend upon him the way she had.

Meaning he needed that formality. That austere uniform of his.

She watched him cross to the fire and stand there, as if gathering his thoughts.

It poked at her, that he did not seem to have a casual setting. That there was only this. Valentino Bonaparte, the dutiful heir. Picture-perfect in every way.

Oddly enough, though she understood all the pressures that could lead to living that way, watching him wear the weight of it made her want to weep.

"These are the things that will occur," he told her, in a quiet voice that was a lot like that voice he'd used on that dreadful morning after. So certain. So terrible. "We will marry, and quickly. It is regrettable that there will be inevitable speculation about the nature of our relationship these past few years. There already has been, as I'm sure you're aware, following the wedding."

"I have spent absolutely no time at all following anyone's thoughts on what happened that day," Carliz said, sharply. "It might surprise you to learn that your wedding and what happened after was not something that I wish to relive."

Something flashed across his stern face and the ache in her intensified. But when he shot her one of those dark, compelling looks of his, she did not falter.

"What astounds me," he said, sounding more and more as if he was actually having a feeling by the moment, "is that I go out of my way to live as blameless a life as possible. I have tried in every arena to act with honor, respect, and dignity. And yet, through no fault of my own, I am consistently and repeatedly dragged back down into a mud not of my own making."

"Yes," Carliz murmured with entirely false sympathy. "Poor little billionaire. What a tragedy it is to have even one moment of one day that is outside of your express control."

The look he shot her then, all affront and astonishment, might have made her laugh on another day. But she was too churned up inside. There was too much happening, here in this quiet room, where she wanted more than anything else to scream.

But she locked that away inside, because she didn't want to give him the satisfaction.

Or maybe she was afraid that if she started screaming, she wouldn't stop.

It began to occur to her that maybe she had not been getting over him the way she'd thought she had been. That maybe all of that gray listlessness had been grief and mourning, not simply a new state of being.

But none of that mattered now.

"In any case," he said, biting off his words, "we will get married here. I will not add an illegitimate child to the list of—"

"The list of what?" she asked, maybe a little sharply. "Slings and arrows thrust upon you, not of your own making? Because that's not how I remember that night, Valentino."

She was certain that she had intended to be civilized. But there was something about the fact that he was mad that wrecked all of her good intentions. If there'd been a heavy enough object nearby, she rather thought she would have flung it straight at his head.

"The doctors say you're in your second trimester.

But all is well." His jaw tensed. His nostrils flared. "I am glad."

"Yes. Noticeably glad, I'd say. The kind of gladness that fills whole rooms."

"We will have to fashion the appropriate contracts," he said then, sounding almost bored. And when that opaque mask settled onto his features once again, she felt it like a hand around her throat. Choking her. Leaving her feeling claustrophobic. Her fingers twitched with the urge to go stick her fingers into that mask, like maybe she could peel it away. As if it was made of a hard plastic and not simply his will.

"Yes, naturally, there will be contracts," she agreed. "I'm sure you will have a great many offensive clauses for the palace's legal team to object to. But there is another wrinkle." He only stared back at her, as if daring her to continue. For some reason, that made her feel... Almost merry. "I am a princess of Las Sosegadas, as you know. That means that I cannot legally marry anyone without the permission of the sovereign."

"That is archaic."

"So are monarchies. Literally." Carliz shrugged. "Mila has always assured me that she will give me no quarrel in this area, but then, you are a special case. I suspect she already dislikes you."

"I have never met your sister."

"No, but I am her baby sister. And according to all the tabloids, you broke my heart. It's possible she holds a grudge." She sighed as if, upon consideration, she liked his chances even less. "She is a just and fair-minded queen but she does hold a wicked personal grudge, it has to be said."

"Everything I have ever heard about your sister suggests she is eminently practical," Valentino replied, in that tone of great authority, as if the things he'd heard were more correct than her lived experience as Queen Emilia's best friend and only true confidante. "I doubt very much that she is interested in the kind of scandal that will ensue if her sister to have a child out of wedlock."

"Maybe," Carliz said airily, because that was more likely to annoy him than if she exploded in temper the way she wanted to do. "Then again, it might make me more relatable. That's of great concern to the palace these days. *Relatability.* Mila is forever weighing how to appear approachable, yet iconic. All at the same time."

"Then I suggest you call her right now," Valentino said, in that silken threat of a voice. His pale gaze moved over her like fire. "And explain to her that she has two options. She can cheerfully approve your marriage or she can oppose it. If it is the former, felicitations will abound on all sides. If it is the latter, you will be legally married in every single country on the planet... except hers."

He let that sink in, in case she was tempted to misunderstand what he meant.

"I'll be sure to make her well aware that you said that," Carliz told him.

And in the end, that wasn't even necessary. Mila laughed when Carliz called. "I knew it," she said with the sort of glee she never showed in public. "And I'm not even going to ask you about complicated timing, overlaps with previous brides-to-be, or any of the rest of it. The heart will do as it pleases."

"I hope that's how you explain it to Mother."

Her sister laughed again, and Carliz almost felt as if things might be all right. At last. "Absolutely not. I am not taking that bullet for you, my darling sister. You will have to tell her yourself."

"Or she can find out in the papers like everyone else." Carliz laughed too, and it was if surrendering to a little levity changed everything, even the sullen British weather outside. She could see a bit of sunshine out there, trying wanly to illuminate a hedge or two in the garden. "I can't wait to hear if she finds Valentino Bonaparte *appropriate*."

"No one will ever be good enough for you," Mila said, her serene voice uncharacteristically absent, then. She sounded fierce. She sounded like a big sister. "Such a man can never and will never exist. So what I hope is that this time, Valentino has taken some time to reflect on his good luck that you will have him. And how little he deserves it."

"I will be certain to let him know," Carliz whispered.

Then she sat there in the reception room over the garden where he'd left her to make her call, staring about sightlessly. Because Mila had undone her. Effortlessly.

Her sister had not used or breathed the word *scandal*. She had not reminded Carliz of her promise never to embarrass the crown. She had acted as if this was all... perfectly reasonable and worth being happy about, even.

It made Carliz want to lie down somewhere and cry.

But she had no time for that, because she was in this strange old house that felt stuffed full of Valentino's presence even when he wasn't in the same room. She stood then, feeling far shakier than she'd like. For a moment she thought she might swoon like some overset princess of yore, felled by nothing at all, but then she remembered. She'd flown into Italy the previous night so she could catch the early tide and walk out to the island. She'd been so agitated, or what she had chosen to call *determined*, that she'd merely gulped down a few biscotti and set out.

She was starving. Not swooning and fainting because she was overcome by emotion.

Not yet, anyway.

Carliz put her hand over her belly and massaged the little bit of roundness that seemed obvious and prominent to her. It told her there was a baby in there, as odd as that seemed to her.

Though the oddness didn't keep her from that fierce rush of love she'd felt the moment she'd known. Before she'd let herself think about the practicalities.

That love grew stronger by the day and fiercer by the minute.

"Don't you worry," she murmured to her bump. "It doesn't matter if your father is terrible. He will do his duty by you." She shook her head at that, hating the bitter way that the words sat in her mouth. "But I will love you enough for both of us, I promise."

And she felt somehow cheered by that, no matter her emotions. They were buffeting her like one storm after the next and had been since that grotty toilet stall in

New York. The reason she felt shaky *now* wasn't those emotions. It wasn't that she was in Valentino's presence, because she had been all day.

This was pure physiology and that felt a bit like a reprieve. She was a pregnant woman who needed food, the end.

She picked her way through the house, back to the kitchen, and slowed as she entered. Because Valentino was there. He was dark and tall and gorgeous, and aggressively male simply because he was *him*. But the truly astonishing thing was that he appeared to be… *cooking*, though she found her brain could not accept that as a possibility.

"You must be hungry," he said gruffly. Almost angrily, as if she was being hungry *at* him—

But she stopped herself from that train of thought. She had a sudden memory of her father from back when she'd been nothing but a naughty teenager. Her group of friends had gotten in a little bit too much trouble at boarding school and Carliz had been called before the king to account for herself, which she had done. But in a manner far too flippant for his taste.

He had shouted at her. And while he was not averse to expressing his disappointment in her in as many ways as possible, always hoping she might listen and shape up, he had never been the kind of man who *shouted*. She had been stunned into silence.

The king had sighed and pressed his fingers to one temple. *You could have been hurt*, he had said quietly. *And it is easier to be angry about that than to accept the fact that sometimes, Carliz, your disregard for your own safety terrifies me.*

She couldn't get that out of her mind. She watched Valentino's crisp, economical movements as he chopped things and then swept them into a bowl, moving around this kitchen as if he spent a great deal of time preparing food for himself here.

Maybe he wasn't angry at her. Maybe he was simply scared, as anyone would be. Of the future. Of this new life they were going to have to do their best to raise well. Or of the two of them together, for that matter. Married to each other. Somehow figuring out how to build a life from all these bright, painful scraps of *almost* that they'd been running from for so long.

Maybe he didn't know how to speak of these things.

And could she blame him? Neither did she.

Carliz went and slid onto one of the stools set on the other side of the counter, blinking when she needed more room than usual. Then smiling at that, because it would not be long before her belly impeded her from sitting in all kinds of places in the way she was used to.

It would be only one of many changes, one right after the next, resulting in the birth of a small human who would change everything even more, and irrevocably.

The truth was that it was impossible to really imagine. It was impossible to speculate on the magnitude of that change.

So instead, she said, "I'm very hungry, as a matter of fact. Thank you."

He had taken off his jacket and rolled up his shirt sleeves to cook, and there was something unbearable about it. Something so beautiful and poignant in the sight of his exposed forearms. All of those astonishing muscles coming together to do something so parochial as cook a meal.

"Someday I will take cooking lessons," she told him, as if she was making a confession. "I've always wanted to. I cooked a very little bit when I lived in halls at university. I can make a mean Bolognese, I want you to know. But I've always wanted to be the sort of person who can open a cupboard, scan the available ingredients, and come up with a whole meal. All of it delicious and bordering on gourmet."

"I was taught that cooking for oneself is a life skill," he said, though his voice…changed as he said that. As if he hadn't meant to say anything.

"I'm surprised to hear that." Carliz sighed happily when he slid a pair of dishes in front of her. One plate sported a fluffy omelet smothered in bright, cheerful vegetables. On the other was a stack of buttered toast. "I would have thought you had nearly as much staff as I did, growing up."

He stood across from her, bracing himself against the counter, but it was his expression that stopped her midbite.

"Our housekeeper made it a game," he said quietly, though not in that controlled quiet way he had. This was much rougher. "When I was young, I often played in the kitchens. I learned how to cook and to clean, all skills she assured me would serve me well no matter my station in life."

"She sounds like a wise woman," Carliz said, but

carefully, because there was a stillness about him that she didn't understand. And a kind of bitterness in his gaze. "For here you are, capable of producing a fine meal at the drop of a hat, all on your own. I promise you that I cannot do the same."

"Ginevra made me think that she taught me these things for my own good," Valentino said, and now the bitterness was in his voice, too. "But she did not. It was all a part of the sick games I did not even realize were being played all around me. So yes, Carliz, I can cook. But what I taste is betrayal no matter what spices I use."

She thought he would turn and stalk off at that, but he didn't. He pushed back from the counter, shifting back until he could lean against the cupboards and cross his arms.

Carliz had seen him stand like that before. It never boded well.

"I take it your sister was amenable." It wasn't really a question.

Carliz returned to the task of eating, though she could no longer taste the food. There were too many questions whirling around in her head and more, she *felt* for him. She wanted to go to him and offer him comfort for the childhood that still brought him pain—but she knew he would not accept it. Not from her, not from anyone.

That made her feel for him even more deeply.

She forced herself to take a few bites, then picked up the linen napkin he'd placed by her plate and pressed it to her mouth. "Mila was lovely about the whole thing," she said as she lowered the napkin. "She never mentioned the scandal of it, though I know that must be a consideration. And I know that is your primary consideration. But I think there are other things that we should consider."

Carliz could sense his disapproval, though that closed-off expression didn't change. "Such as?"

"Maybe, Valentino, just maybe, I don't want to marry a man who doesn't like me at all," she said quietly. "A man who has spent the bulk of what can only loosely be called our relationship doing his best to get away from me. Why would I want to marry a man like that?"

To her surprise, he smiled.

It was a dark thing, a hard curve of sensual and stern lips.

But it was hardwired deep into all the parts of her she'd been so sure had frozen into disuse over the past three months. She'd been so sure it would never again be a factor, having learned her lesson at last.

She had been wrong about that. Very wrong. Because one little smile, one little spark, and she was engulfed in flames once again.

"I can think of at least one excellent reason to marry me, *Principessa*," Valentino said in that low, stirring way of his. "Do you need me to remind you what that is?"

CHAPTER SEVEN

VALENTINO MARRIED PRINCESS CARLIZ in the front room of his house in London.

It was an excessively well-appointed room, but it was not the famous cathedral in her kingdom that her sister would marry in, one day. It was not the lovely old chapel on the island where he had been set to marry last summer.

Carliz wore a quiet dress in a pale hue that was not quite white and did not smile. He wore a suit and presented her with a spectacular ring that had been his mother's, which, upon reflection was perhaps ill-suited for a union that he did not intend to let fall apart the way his parents had.

But when he kissed her, sealing their union, it was an unremarkable brush of lips and yet still that dark thrill rushed through him. That same insatiable need.

He already regretted that he'd had no choice but to make this decision.

"Will we be taking a honeymoon?" Princess Carliz, *his wife*, asked in that tone she'd taken with him over the past fortnight that they'd stayed here in London, sorting out contracts and wedding arrangements.

It was edgier by the day. Too sharp, and that dark look in her usually gleaming eyes. "I can't wait to sit somewhere lovely in this same towering fury. It's love's young dream, I dare say."

"We will return to the island," he told her in freezing tones, and not because she was being provoking. But because all he could think of was that laughably quick brush of their lips. How could something haunt him when it had barely happened? "And we will iron out the contours of this bargain we've made."

"What a marvelous idea," she murmured dryly, holding her wedding flowers before her like a shield. Or a weapon designed to make him feel small, and he did not like that the happy little blossoms managed it when no one else had since he was, in fact, small. "Thank you so much for asking my opinion on the matter."

"We will leave in the morning," he gritted out.

Then he left her there to spend his wedding night in his club, fully aware that she had been his wedding night once before. At least this time he'd actually gone ahead and made the damned vows.

The Diamond Club was the sort of place where he ought to have been able to shrug off his cares and worries alike. That had been the point of it, in the beginning. It was exclusive and elite, invitation only, so that only the ten wealthiest people in all of the world were allowed to hold membership.

He liked everything about the place. The clubhouse itself was on a discreet and quiet street not far from his house in London. He kept a suite there, for he had often stayed at the club when he did not wish to be tracked by the paparazzi or anyone else. The staff was almost supernaturally excellent, capable of anticipating every whim almost before it was formed. Though Valentino had found the place had lost quite a bit of its luster once he realized that his brother was also a member.

He'd preferred the days before he'd known that, when he'd simply come and gone by helicopter, in and out of his private suite, never setting eyes on anyone but the fearsomely well-trained manager, Lazlo, who made everyone he encountered feel as if he worked only and ever for them.

Tonight, however, he did not wish to be alone in his suite. He tried to tell himself that he had removed himself from his house because his marriage was a sham and he cared nothing at all for the woman he'd married or anything else involving her, but that was how he'd expected to feel three months ago. Should he have actually married Francesca.

Had he felt that way tonight, he would have seen no reason to leave the house.

He had left because if he didn't, then that pounding, driving need inside him would take him over. It had already begun. He had stood there in the aftermath of their small ceremony, vowing to himself that he would not touch her again.

But what was he trying to prove? What new hair shirt was this, when he thought he was well used to the closetful he already knew too well—and could identify now, thanks to her.

Especially when he had shamelessly used the fire that

always burned between them to get Carliz to marry him in the first place.

He assumed she would have married him one way or the other, eventually, or she wouldn't have gotten on his plane back in Italy. But he hadn't needed to mount any arguments. He hadn't had to offer her an object lesson in why they needed to get married in the first place. He had simply raised his brow and waited.

She had sat there in his kitchen, her cheeks getting redder and her eyes getting brighter.

He was sure that the whole of his house smelled of cinnamon, now.

I will marry you, she had said solemnly, as if there had ever been any doubt.

Valentino had told himself that the triumph he'd felt then was a simple thing. That it had nothing to do with any primitive need to possess her in any and every way he could, because he refused to accept that need existed in him.

It was simply the pleasure of a good deal well negotiated, he'd told himself.

But if that were true, there was no reason why a simple brush of lips at their wedding should haunt him out from his house and into the streets of London. There was no reason why the clatter and roar of the city should fade as he walked, because all he could seem to think about was the way she'd looked at him, those eyes of her like ancient treasure, as she'd recited her vows.

He could not see how more time alone in his head would help.

Once he got to the club, he went to one of the club's

main rooms and nodded at a few familiar faces, though he did not stop to talk to anyone. It was enough to have his favorite drink waiting when he took his preferred seat. It was enough to page through the *Times* like some or other duke from centuries past.

It was enough to sit in the place, a monument to a certain kind of power, and remind himself that he was the one who had it. His wife—*his wife*—was a princess, true enough. But only one of them did the kneeling—

Stop, he growled at himself, outraged that even here he was not free of her. That nowhere was safe.

And when someone sat down in the chair beside him, despite the many empty and available spots around the soothingly lit room, he scowled.

Then all the harder when he realized it was Aristide.

It was all very well for someone like Aristide to speak of change. To pretend it was possible.

That did not mean it was.

Or that Valentino might wish to take part in it.

"I do not recall inviting you to sit," Valentino said after a baleful moment. "But then, you have never needed an invitation to intrude upon me, have you?"

There was a time when his brother would have taken that bait, but tonight Aristide only smirked. "Surely you must exhaust yourself with all of the expected snide comments, brother. Besides, it is all very boring. If you must insult me, is it too much to ask that you come up with something new?"

"If I had wanted conversation, I would have addressed my mirror," Valentino replied coldly. "That would have provided me with far more opportunity for reflection and honest interchange than whatever games it is you think you will be playing with me tonight."

And they stared at each other, all of that tangled history between them.

"I thought you should know," Aristide said after a moment, in a sort of deeply calm voice that Valentino did not associate with his reckless brother at all. There was a certainty there. A *settled* quality that made no sense, but that Valentino could see all over him. It was even in the way he sat. "It is early days, but Francesca and I are expecting a child."

Valentino stared back at him. "Why are you telling me this?"

"I appreciate your congratulations." Aristide shook his head. "In the past, you have had a tendency to assume the worst, so I thought you should know. My wife and I are having a baby. It is not an assault on you, or your position as heir—whatever that means with a father such as ours. I merely thought you should hear it from me."

Valentino studied his brother, his fingers clenched tighter than they should have been around his drink. "It is funny, is it not, that you have anointed yourself the messenger of all of these things. That despite the reception you must expect from me, you consider it your duty to fill me in. What does that say about you, I wonder?"

"Perhaps nothing," his brother said quietly. "But then, I am the one who trusted you to remain my friend no matter what happened. You are the one who broke that trust."

But there was not any of the bitterness there that had

been, once. Valentino could not account for the difference. It made him…uneasy.

"Your mother taught me to cook and clean as a child," Valentino said instead, abruptly. "Do you remember?"

"Of course I remember," Aristide said, and when he shifted in his chair he was the lounging, reckless creature he had always been. As if Valentino had imagined the change. Or as if this was a mask his brother wore, not unlike his own—but he dismissed that. "I was there."

"Why?" Valentino asked, aware that he sounded much more fierce than necessary. "Why did she do such a thing? Was it…did she get some amusement from this?"

He detested himself for asking. But then he didn't know why the only thing he could think to do after receiving the report from his doctor—the confirmation that Carliz really was having his baby, which *he* knew meant she would not be walking away from him—was cook for her.

Just as he couldn't understand why he'd told her about Ginevra and her cooking classes in the first place. About a period in his life he did his best to pretend had never occurred. Because he remembered all too well when he and Aristide had been friends. And how that had ended, when he'd discovered that most of his family had been lying to him all along.

He expected his brother to scoff. To toss off one of his trademark witticisms.

Maybe he wanted Aristide to do exactly that. To remind him that no matter the few good memories he had of his childhood, they had always been lies. That Aristide's take on that time would only be a part of those lies.

But Aristide only looked back at him with a curious sort of look on his face. For the life of him, Valentino could not interpret it.

"Cooking and cleaning is how my mother loves, Valentino," Aristide told him, a little too kindly for Valentino's taste. "It is how she shows her love. Not quite the villain in your story, I think. Just a woman in love. For her sins."

Something within Valentino seemed to crack wide open at that. He stood, leaving his drink untasted.

"I commend you on your ill-gotten marriage and all the many moral lessons it will teach an impressionable child," he said. And then, "As it happens, I have also married. And I'm also expecting a child."

Something flashed in Aristide's eyes, though it looked a lot like resignation. "But of course you are."

Valentino stood. "May the cycle continue."

He had said such things to his brother before. This was nothing new. But for the first time, he didn't feel the usual sting as he walked away. Usually there was a level of outrage, but it was always held up by his absolute certainty that he was in the right. That he was the good one. That he had always behaved as he should.

But if cooking and cleaning were how Ginevra showed love, and it was not simply her job… If she had taught Valentino this language as well as her own son…

He did not care for the direction of his thoughts.

It was as if something in him was shifting, changing against his will, and he did not like it.

He took his time walking through the streets of London with the wet in his face, as if that might sort him out. It was late when he shouldered his way into the tidy old house and started for the stairs, somehow unsurprised when Carliz appeared at the top of them.

As if he'd summoned her.

Dressed in nothing but a chemise because she clearly wanted him mad and desperate, and it worked.

"I thought you were out carousing," she said coolly, down her nose and down the stairs. "The way all bridegrooms traditionally do on their wedding night as it sets such a delightful precedent for the marriage, I am sure."

"It is still our wedding night, *mia principessa*."

And he released himself from the vows he'd made after the ceremony in that moment. Because he and Carliz had made their own vows today, had they not? And who was Valentino to deny the power of an ancient ritual?

With my body, he had told her, *I thee worship*.

He thought it was about time he started.

"Is this a wedding night at all?" she asked dryly, but there was a certain glimmer in that burnished gold gaze of hers. A knowing spark. "How would I be able to tell?"

He started up the stairs toward her, something dark and needy taking him over more and more with every step.

"Never fear," he told her. "I'll show you."

And so he did.

He advanced upon her, his heartbeat a match for the fire he could see in her gaze. By the way her eyes widened as he came ever closer, and best of all, the fact that she did not move out of the way. Not by so much as a hair.

When he got to the top of the stair he simply hauled her to him, set his mouth to hers, and carried her, once more, to the nearest bed.

That was where he took his time, unwrapping her like the gift he undoubtedly did not deserve.

It had been a long three months. And she had been a virgin, which meant that he, who had never claimed any kind of ownership over any of his lovers, was the only one to have ever possessed her.

That knowledge worked in him like something mad, impossible, overwhelming. Some kind of virus taking over each and every cell and bone and organ. He could feel the way it infected him. He could feel it rush through him, making him feel near enough to unworthy that it was as if he was someone else entirely.

Someone he doubted very much he would like on the other side of this spiral down into sheer madness.

But he couldn't stop.

He didn't *want* to stop.

What he wanted was to make that sense of possession real.

Valentino reacquainted himself with every curve, every sweet plane. He found that thickening at her waist, her newly rounded belly, and felt something shake in him—deep.

If anything, the new intensity of her curves made her even more beautiful. The fact that she had married him, that she was carrying his child—he didn't have to like how those things had come to pass, and he didn't have to have the faintest romanticized notion of how things between them would go.

He was a man. She was a woman. And they had created a life between them.

Valentino would have to be the kind of monster his own father was, the kind of monster he'd dedicated the whole of his life to *not* being, not to care about something like that.

But this was not the time to think of monsters. This was a time to remind Carliz not only who he was, but who she was. And who they were together.

This was a time to find his way back to that glazed, bright glory in her gaze when she looked at him. The way her lips parted as if she was too oversensitive to breathe. The way she obeyed his every command.

Not, he knew, because she was somehow incapable of standing up for herself. Had she not proven that already?

"You like it when I tell you what to do," he said, his voice a low growl, when he finally moved her to sit astride him so he could gaze upon her as if she were something like a fertility goddess.

Because she was. She was *his* fertility goddess, and he nearly lost himself then.

"I promise that I will always do what you tell me to do," Carliz whispered throatily, a knowing little smile on her lips. "Just as long as we are naked."

He laughed, a low, dark sort of sound, and then he drove into her. She shattered at once, throwing her head back and crying out his name, and he knew.

She had given him the key to this puzzle.

He would make this work, after all.

This most unlikely of unions, which should surely have led him straight to disaster, would be all right.

All he needed to do was keep his princess wife as naked as possible.

CHAPTER EIGHT

THE SECOND TRIMESTER was much better than the first. Carliz felt like herself again.

Though it was hard to say if that was the simple benefit of being in a different part of her pregnancy, or if it was all to do with the marriage she'd somehow found herself in.

It was as if their wedding night had pried the lid off at last. She'd woken up the next morning, convinced that he was going to do the same thing he'd done after their first night together. They had started off in one of his guest rooms, because it was closest to where she'd stood at the top of the stairs when he'd come in. And then, because he'd been in that sort of mood, he had declared that they might as well introduce the rest of the house to its new lady.

So they had, until dawn.

She'd woken up in what he'd told her was his bed when he was in London, and there was no particular reason that she should feel such a thrill at that. She was married to him now. *Married.* It was likely going to be her bed, too.

Or maybe not, something in her whispered, because

it had dawned on her that it was happening again. She was alone, again. He had left her to wake up without him, *again*.

That had not gone well the last time.

She had taken her time getting ready in the clothes she had sent on from the hotel she'd intended to stay in down in Italy, licking her wounds and planning a different life.

Naturally, instead, you married him, she'd muttered to herself.

Carliz had taken great care with her appearance that first day as his wife. If he was going to turn into stone again the way he seemed to do come morning, she'd intended to make it hard for him. She'd intended to make it hurt.

Because one thing had become abundantly clear during the long hours of the night. There hadn't been any spankings this time, but that was not to say that he'd gone any easier on her.

She would have been disappointed if he had.

Valentino Bonaparte was the only man alive who had ever treated her like she was *strong*. Not just pretty. Not just pedigreed. But fully capable of taking anything he chose to give her, then giving it back to him so that they both could benefit.

It was the loveliest cycle she'd ever been a part of.

And she'd understood, at last, that this was what he'd seen in her when they'd first met in Rome. This all-consuming hunger. This specific need that could only be doused for a little while, and only by surrendering themselves to each other again and again and again.

It had no longer been a surprise to her that he had walked away from it. That was likely the smarter path to take. Not the one she took, however.

When she'd dressed herself, done her hair, and fixed her makeup so she looked effortlessly sultry, she'd started down the stairs to face him anyway. Because the most important things she'd learned over the course of the night was that she hadn't made up a single thing that had happened between them. Not one thing. He had felt everything she had. He had experienced it all the same way that she had.

The only difference was that he had chosen to walk away from it. Then had acted as if he'd had no idea why she might want to rush straight in anyway.

Carliz had known better, at last. It didn't matter what he said. It didn't even really matter what he did, not while he had all those clothes on, all those bespoke suits that were really just deliciously tailored armor against his feelings.

The only truth that mattered was the truth they made between them, tangled up in each other, skin to skin.

She'd vowed that she wasn't going to forget that again.

Yet when she'd marched into that kitchen where she was still amazed that this man of all men actually *cooked for himself*, she'd stopped dead.

Because he had not been wearing one of those suits that morning. He had been standing there at his counter, wearing nothing but a pair of deeply fascinating boxer briefs that molded to one of her favorite parts of his body. He had been typing into a slick laptop that he'd cracked open before him. And he'd spared her a short, thrilling glance. "You should eat, *Principessa*," he had told her with only the faintest hint of admonishment. "You must think of the baby."

Then he'd indicated, with a tilt of his head, the plates of food that had waited for her on the table out closer to the garden.

Even weeks later and in a different country, remembering that first morning of their married life made her break out all over in happy little goose bumps.

There had been somewhat less giddy conversations with the palace. Her mother had been torn between outrage that Carliz had essentially gone off and eloped, histrionic concern at what that would *do* to the royal family's *image*, and obvious, unadulterated delight that *one* of her daughters had actually taken that step into matrimony.

Though the fact that the baby would come much too early, by even the most casual calculations, about put her over the edge.

No longer so heartbroken, I hope, Mila had said, on one of the occasions that the two of them spoke privately.

Hearts are amazing organs, Carliz had replied, which wasn't answering the question and they both knew it. *So much hardier than they seem. And somehow able to thrive in the most complicated scenarios.*

Just remember, her sister had said with that serene smile of hers. *If you bring him back home, I can throw him into the palace dungeon at will.*

The team that had been put together to find Carliz a husband were clearly less delighted, but the head aide spoke to her politely enough.

In the end, the woman said after a lengthy interrogation about the actual nature of her relationship with Valentino, including dates and hard truths, *you will be far more likely to behave if you're happy.*

I'm sure that's true of everyone, Carliz had replied. *And just as unlikely.*

Your sister does not require happiness, the aide had said. *She will behave no matter what. So you see, in our office where we dislike surprises, this is not so bad.* The older woman had leveled a look at her and though Carliz braced herself, she had not rolled into a lecture. Instead, she'd smiled and looked…kind. *And for all your mother's clucking, this is also not the Dark Ages. Congratulations on the next prince or princess of the realm, Your Highness.*

And it had surprised Carliz how much that had affected her. How much it had meant and continued to mean.

Just as it surprised her that now, when her duty to the crown was both assured and no longer a pressing issue, she felt something like homesick. Not for the grayness or the heaviness of those first three months, but what she missed were those nights with her sister. Getting to spend time with Mila the way they had when they were little girls, and even then, only rarely. Because Mila's destiny had always been assured and silly games with her sister had never been part of her studies.

Carliz knew that she would never regret those otherwise sad months for that time with her sister alone.

Living on a private island off the coast of Italy, of

course, was not exactly the worst thing she'd ever had
to endure.

Especially because Valentino kept right on treating
her like dessert. And it turned out that the man had a
sweet tooth that only Carliz could assuage.

He found her wherever she was. Sitting with her feet
in the pool, wandering the gardens, reading a book. He
was insatiable and better still, he was uninhibited in the
extreme. He took her everywhere, in every possible way,
until her days were shot through with sensuality like
burning red threads that held everything else together.

His days were always filled with work, so he would
call her into his offices and conduct whole calls while
she stood there, naked before him. Sometimes he made
her pleasure herself in the chair before his desk, her feet
propped up so he could see everything while she tipped
back her head, slipped her hands between her thighs,
and did as he liked. As he commanded.

Other times he had her kneel before him and pleasure
him while he tended to what he called the most tedious
part of his life, his paperwork.

Her job was to keep him just on edge enough that
he could continue to work. Just close enough so that he
was not leveled by the need to make love to her mouth
with that same inexhaustible self-control that made her
shatter apart without him having to even lay a finger
upon her.

She failed every time.

And she rather thought that was the point.

Carliz had been in Italy for near on a month when
the rest of her things arrived, sent with love and cour-

tesy from the palace. And it felt strange all over again to see her belongings hanging in the dressing room that adjoined Valentino's. It was odd to have a whole sitting room allocated for her use with its pretty little terrace that looked out toward the sea, and now the tables held the small trinkets she'd picked up in her travels.

It was an odd thing indeed to no longer be Valentino's assumed affair, his dramatic estranged love, but his wife. She wasn't sure she knew how to take on the role of a wife. She'd been much better at manufacturing the story of the first version of them.

Possibly because, for all the ways she knew this man as well as she knew herself, there were a lot of other ways she didn't know him at all.

There were rules about where she could walk on the island, for example. She was not to stray onto his brother's property, ever. Much less visit his father.

"I will take care of that unpleasant duty when I must," Valentino told her. "I'd prefer it if he never laid eyes on you at all."

But he had told her that in bed and she'd still been addled by the number of orgasms she'd had. The pure magic that man could work with his fingers and his tongue. So she hadn't argued.

She liked to think that had he told her at a different time, she might have.

At a dinner in her second month on the island, he waved the subject of his father away.

"The man has nothing to add to anything but malice," he said dismissively. "He is a poison, nothing more. The only way I know how to deal with him is a campaign of failing to react no matter how outrageous he becomes. I'm not sure that I'll be able to do that if I'm also protecting you from his usual snide barbs."

That sounded so reasonable. But Carliz couldn't help noticing that his punctuation to that statement was to take her there, across the table, in a blistering rush of passion that left her panting, a little bit dizzy, and with her concerns unaddressed.

She began to put those things together. If she looked back, ever since their wedding night, he had responded to pretty much everything in precisely the same way. Sex.

When she had asked him what, exactly, was the root of his dispute with his brother—a rivalry so intense that the whole world knew of it—he had said something offhanded, then commanded her to strip. When she had asked about his mother, having seen a portrait of her in the gallery, he had swung her up into his arms, carried her into one of the nearby rooms, and tied her to the sofa.

In fact, she thought when she woke one morning after a typically long and glorious night in his arms, she could not think of a single real conversation they'd had.

Not one. And it made her feel foolish. Which she supposed she was meant to feel. Because that was what he was doing. He was playing her for a fool. He was doing it deliberately.

She wasn't sure how she had failed to notice.

Carliz swung out of the bed and snatched up the little silk wrapper that she wore, because he liked it. That annoyed her too, and she was frowning as she stalked out into the rest of what she supposed was *their* suite.

Though now that she was paying attention, it was clear that the room set aside for her use was as far away from his as possible.

Another thing she hadn't noticed, because all she really cared about was where he was at any given moment and how quickly he could be inside her.

She left the suite and walked as regally as possible down the stairs, smiling in the best approximation of her sister's serenity as she passed staff members who she usually did not appear in front of in nothing but a silk wrapper. She marched herself across the house and straight into Valentino's office, standing there before his desk until he deigned to look up at her, one dark brow already aloft.

"Do you need me to teach you some manners again, *mia principessa*?"

She might be mad at him, but that did nothing to change the way her body reacted to him. It was as if he flipped a switch in her. As if that was all it took. One slightly suggestive statement and her whole body was vibrating like a tuning fork.

"You're avoiding me," she accused him.

"How can this be so?" he asked idly. "We are always together."

"I don't mean physically."

"My dear princess wife," he said, and suddenly everything was silk and heat, and his gaze crowded into her like he was already thrusting home between her legs. "You are standing much too far away from me."

And it felt almost like an out-of-body experience, because she was aware of what he was doing this time.

It was as if she was watching it from somewhere else. The way he rose and came around his desk to take her in his arms. The way he kissed her, so deep, so stirring, that there was nothing she could do but kiss him back with all she was and everything she had.

Carliz was both there and not there as he brought her down with him into that thick rug before the fire in his office, took his time stripping that wrapper from her body, and feasted on her until she had her fingers sunk deep in his hair and was sobbing out his name the way she always did.

And then again, louder still, when he set her before him on her hands and knees in deference to her growing belly and took her from behind, reaching up to pull her head around so he could kiss her in that same deep, restless way.

Until there was nothing to do but surrender as he took her apart.

But in the aftermath, she came back to herself, and this time, remembered. So she turned to him as they lay there and traced the stern lines of his face with a fingertip.

"It's so hard to believe we get to be together like this after all those years of running away from these feelings," she said.

She was close to him, and she was watching for it, so she saw the way he stiffened. It was almost imperceptible, but she saw it.

Carliz pushed on. "Do you know, when I first laid eyes on you, I don't think I ever truly imagined that this could happen. That we would get this day in and day out. Husband and wife, falling more and more in love—"

There was a part of her that wanted to tell herself that she was only testing him by saying that word, but he'd been fooling her quite enough. She didn't see why she needed to fool herself. Carliz had been in love with this man since the moment she'd laid eyes on him.

That was simply the way it was. The way it always had been.

But he sat up, disentangling himself from the heat they'd made. And the stern way he looked at her was not in the least bit sexy.

"I will thank you," he said, very quietly, "not to speak about your feelings in my presence."

"I will speak about whatever I want, Valentino," she replied in the same deceptively soft way. "I'm sorry if my love offends you. But I feel fairly certain that, given the fact you've been running from it since that night in Rome, you've been fully aware that it's been here, all along."

"I want you to hear me, Carliz." He stood then, leaving her sitting naked on the floor, surrounded by a wrapper of silk. And she couldn't seem to move as he dressed, quickly, betraying absolutely no emotion when she was certain she could feel it coming off of him in waves. "I know you have a tendency to hear what you wish to hear. And make up scenarios to suit the ones you already have in your head."

"Yes," she agreed dryly. "I'm clearly delusional. That's why I'm your wife. I hallucinated my way here."

"The chemistry between us is off the charts," he said

coolly, and she hated him for that. Quantifying it seemed to cheapen it, and she didn't want *chemistry*. She certainly didn't want *off the charts* chemistry. Not when she knew that this was so much more than that.

And that he was only saying that because he was trying to diminish what it *really* was.

"I think what you mean is that you're in love with me," she said, because she knew he was. It was the intensity between them, she supposed. It was the fact he'd told her they could never be anything and now they were married. It could be because her life had always been glossy, but empty, and he had felt like the only real thing in it since Rome. It was because she was there when he held her close. She was there when he stared at her as if no one but them existed. She was here, now. She could feel what was between them and she wasn't afraid to name it. But that didn't make it easier to say. Because it certainly wasn't something he wanted to hear. "And that doesn't have to be scary, Valentino, because I'm in love with you too."

"I am not in love with you," he told her, and was all the more brutal because he looked…patient. Perhaps slightly pitying. There was no flashing in his gaze that she could cling to and call denial. There was no flare of temper in his voice that she could tell herself was the truth of how he really felt.

She thought it would have hurt her less if he'd backhanded her.

Instead, he slipped his hands into his pockets. "I can see that this is distressing you, but I thought we understood each other. I'm happy to have sex with you all day, every day, Carliz. I like sex. I particularly like it with you."

"If you say another word about sex or chemistry," she said, though her throat was tight and her voice sounded strangled, "I will not be responsible for my actions."

Again, that pitying look. "This is what I had hoped to avoid. But I suppose it is better to come to an understanding before our child is born. There will be no scenes in my house." And at least, when he took on that stern, formidable look again, it was better than pity. Anything was better than pity. Though she had to remind herself that he didn't know any better, not this man who'd built himself a mausoleum to reside in while he was still alive. Anything to avoid those feelings he didn't think he had, or the childhood that had made him this way. "Perhaps you have not noticed that everything in this house is precisely calibrated to soothe."

"Like a crypt," she said, and somehow without anything like a sob in her voice. Though she felt like a sob personified, all the same.

"I will not have chaos," he told her, something urgent in the way he spoke. The way he looked at her, even the way he held himself. All those feelings he didn't want, filling him up. *Love*, she thought, and she knew she was right because it hummed in her, deep. "I want the home that I live in to feel like an upscale art gallery, Carliz. Not a bar, filled with drunkards, broken glass, and puddles of regrets on the floor."

She decided this was not the time to break the news to him that babies were not typically mindful of upscale gallery rules.

"You're describing an excellent Friday night," she shot back instead. She had the urge to wrap herself up again, to hide herself from his gaze, but that served him, not her. So instead, she stayed where she was, sitting there like a goddess on a half shell with every bit of royal blood inside of her pumping, hard.

Because she was her sister's heir, like it or not. She could give regal for days.

And she knew perfectly well that for all his talk about chaos and crypts, he didn't have any more control at the sight of her nakedness then she did when she beheld his.

In case she needed more proof that this man who could control everything, and believed he could control his own baby, could not control his heart around her.

"My fear has always been that we are fundamentally incompatible," he told her as if that had weighed heavy on him just moments before, when he had been losing himself between her thighs. "Sexual attraction without shared values is cancerous."

"Or it's fun, Valentino."

"How would you know?" he asked her softly. "You acted the part of the party princess, but it was a lie. A role you played to get attention, and now you have mine, don't you? But you don't want it."

"I do want it. That's what I've tried to—"

"What you want is a person you've made up in your head," he said, a quiet devastation that swiped hard at the confidence in this, in love, in *them* that she was trying so hard to cling to. "And what I wanted was a biddable, quiet wife who would bear no resemblance whatsoever to the black hole of attention-seeking be-havior that was my mother."

If he really had slapped her, she didn't think she could have been more startled. "I have never heard you say a bad word about your mother before."

"Because I never speak of my mother," he bit out, something in his gaze that told her that whatever else this was, this was Valentino without a mask. She'd claimed she wanted that. She did want that. "What would be the point?"

"She was your mother. You don't need a point."

"Tell me if you see the similarities, Carliz." His eyes were blazing now. "She was a happy-go-lucky creature, everyone says so. Renowned for her beauty and vivacity. This is why my father pursued her. Then, as men do, he took her back to his island and turned her into a ghost of herself." His smile was hard. Brutal. "I did not witness this. I only saw the aftermath. The mother who raised me was the woman he made, not the woman he mar-ried. And that woman was jealous. Insecure. She was not pleasant to be around, and then, once the truth was out—confirming what she had suspected for years, only to be told she was mad—she supplemented the worst parts of herself with pills. Alcohol. Whatever was to hand."

"I'm so sorry," Carliz whispered. "You didn't deserve that. She didn't deserve it either."

"Do you want to know the overwhelming feeling that I grapple with day and night?" And now his eyes were flashing, but not in a way she liked. "Guilt. With a healthy dollop of shame. Because when my brother told me the information that should never have been kept secret in the first place, information he knew I should have had already, I wanted to leave. This place, my father, all of it."

He didn't say *and Aristide*. The brother he had clearly been close with, once. She wondered at the omission.

But Valentino was still talking in that same brutal manner. "My mother refused to go. And I watched her wallow in the feelings that had already bested her. For years. Until she finally made herself so ill that she needed a hospital. And my father refused to call for the boat or the helicopter that could have saved her. And I didn't know any of this until too late, because I was tired of her nonsense and sleeping in the old chapel at the base of this hill to get away from all of them. Those, Carliz, are the only feelings I have."

With every word he seemed to loom larger, so he was towering over her now, though he hadn't moved. And his eyes had gone nearly black with the force of what he was telling her. With the force of all those things she could tell that he kept inside him all this time.

"You were a child," she said, trying to sound calm. Centered. "It wasn't your responsibility to care for either one of your parents."

"Once again, how would you know?" His eyes blazed. His mouth was a flat line. "Nothing has ever been expected of you. You were never called upon to do anything at all but smile prettily and keep to the background. What responsibilities have you ever had?"

There it was, she thought dazedly. That backhand she thought she'd like better.

Turned out, she didn't.

"I can appreciate what you're doing now," she said then. And it was harder than anything else she could remember doing, even coming here to tell him about the baby, to remain calm. Or to sound calm, anyway. "You might want to remember that you've already spent years being unkind to me, Valentino. I'm used to it. I don't believe it any more now than I did then."

She had never believed it.

What had bloomed between them had been that strong from the start, like a chain linking them together, but also making it impossible for them to lie to each other no matter what words they used.

But there was more than that.

It was the way he had held her on the dance floor in Rome, as if she was precious. Made of spun glass and wonder. His hands had been so big and yet so gentle at the small of her back. It had been the way he moved with her, smooth and easy, as if he had been holding her in his arms his whole life.

There was the way he had tended to her after their second round that first night. He had carried her into his bath and washed her with his own hands, gentle once again. He had spanked her and she had still been processing how much she'd liked that. He had taken her virginity and she had still been wild with longing and passion and all of that shattering.

Yet he had treated her as if he cherished her.

It had made the next morning all the more devastating.

For a long time—those long three months—she had told herself that the truth of this man was in his hardness, but now she shared a bed with him. She knew the melting softness of the way he held her in the dark. She knew the kisses he brushed over her brow when he thought she was asleep.

She knew the hardness was an expression he used. But Carliz was more certain by the day that the real Valentino was the one he hid.

This only confirmed it.

Though she had to keep telling herself that.

"That doesn't make you heroic, *mia principessa*," he said from between his teeth. "It makes you masochistic."

"But that's what you like most about me," she shot right back.

And this time, she knew that she dared him to put her over his knee. That she wanted him to, if only to prove yet again that they fit each other perfectly.

That she could earn his softness by taking his hardness.

That maybe she was the only one who could.

He met that dare and then exceeded it, spanking her until all of these things she felt about him came pouring out. He spanked her until she sobbed out her pleasure in that sharp, delicious fire, called him names, and then shattered into pieces with his fingers plunged deep inside of her.

Only to feel it all over again when he carried her to that chair, settled her astride him, and gripped her hot, red bottom with his deliberate hands. He built that fire in her back up, then held her there, sobbing for him all over again for what seemed like a lifetime.

And when he finally relented, threw her over the cliff and then followed, she leaned forward and bit him.

Hard enough to leave a mark, right there above his collarbone.

Valentino's eyes glittered as he pressed his fingers to it, some while later. He was watching her closely.

She could only hope she looked as unrepentant as she felt.

"That is the only scenario in which we will discuss *feelings* in this marriage," he told her. "Do you understand?"

"I understand what you said," Carliz replied. "That doesn't constitute agreement."

"I am leaving on a business trip," he told her. "Originally I intended to take you with me, but I think it is best if we put a little space around this, you and I."

She was curled up in the chair and when he handed her the wrapper from the floor, she didn't bother to take it. He hung it on the chair's arm beside her. "Naturally," she murmured in agreement. "You need to get those defenses nice and high again."

"Carliz." And she inhaled, quickly and deeply when he leaned over her and took her chin in his hand, tilting her head back so she had no choice but to fall straight into his gaze. Everything in her melted, the way it always did. Her body wasn't conflicted about him or their marriage at all. Or perhaps it simply wasn't afraid to follow things it wanted, even if it hurt. "I suggest that you spend your time in this house finding something to do with yourself that does not involve poking at me. Because that approach will get you spanked, yes. It will lead to scenes like this one, which are the only scenes I intend to allow. But it will never get you what you want."

But he had said things like that before, hadn't he? And here she was all the same.

Only when she swallowed, filled a powerful sort of sadness—for him, for her—that she couldn't seem to shove away, did he step back. Then she watched him pull himself together so easily. So quickly.

She really did wish she could believe that he was truly that cold, and hate him.

Carliz thought that maybe she could talk herself into it—but in that moment, the strangest sensation took her over. She clapped a hand to her belly, looking down in wonder.

"Is something wrong?" Valentino's voice was gruff. Not that stern, remote detachment that made her want to claw at him, just to see if ice could bleed.

"I think…" It happened again, and she smiled. And she knew. "I think he kicked."

They had found out they were having a son only the week before. In typical form, Valentino had only nodded curtly. Carliz had started singing the baby songs, because now she knew that it was a boy. A baby boy. Her little boy.

That was the sort of beautiful that hurt, but she liked it.

She held her breath as Valentino squatted down beside her. He reached out a hand but stopped before he touched her, looking up to her as if for her permission. And she felt…ancient. As if some deep, wild femininity that she hadn't known until now lived there inside of her. Because in so many things, she was more than happy to follow this man. But this was something she knew. Their future was *inside* of her.

She took his hand and she spread it out over that belly of hers that seemed to grow bigger by the day. By the hour. She watched his face change as that telltale little kick bubbled there beneath his palm.

"He knows his father," she whispered.

And for a moment, she saw a Valentino she had only ever dreamed about. He looked…shattered, but with joy. His eyes changed and there had never been a blue that color, she was sure of it.

He looked down at her belly with wonder, and then he looked at her—

And Carliz watched as he remembered himself. She couldn't seem to breathe as he turned himself back into stone and ice.

Though it seemed to take him longer than it usually did.

"I will be gone ten days," he told her, so matter-of-factly it hurt. "It is my hope that you will use this time wisely. Explore the house, Carliz. This is the place I made to reflect who I am. It is all perfectly obvious. Every single thing I keep in this house is calming. I hope that you can be one of them."

He still had his hands on her belly, and he tightened them, just slightly, as if he was trying to hug his son.

She thought she might cry, but that would be worse. Instead, she forced herself to say nothing. To sit there with the baby they'd made kicking inside her for the first time as Valentino did what he did best and walked away from her again.

But this time, she did not cry. This time, when she stood—her sore bottom reminding her of him with every step—she decided to do exactly what he'd asked.

After he left, she wandered around the house, looking at the whole of it sternly, the way he must.

She saw every bit of minimalism, as if he'd wished to diminish the very things he chose to display. She saw bare walls, likely chosen with that same deliberate hand, that she remembered from London, too, though London retained the character of the original building to give it a cozier feel. This place had been built for starkness. Everything was very spare, which she knew she was meant to find sophisticated.

But she had been raised in a palace, filled with ancient artifacts and national treasures, all of them crammed in so that no era was left out.

And her country was a cold, snowy place. The winters were long and dark.

They liked color in Las Sosegadas. So did Carliz.

So the next morning, she went into the little study they'd set up for her and she took some time to arrange all of her half-finished canvases, replacing the soporific paintings that were already hanging in the suite. Then she gathered up her paints and stepped out into the hall, finally feeling completely at home in this place.

Then she did what she'd been yearning to do all along, and decorated.

Every wall. Every ceiling.

And when the staff begged her to rethink, she simply chose bolder colors.

Carliz worked feverishly, night and day, and when she was done, she had completely transformed Valentino's austere little palace.

She had made it chaotic. Bright. Happy and more than a little whimsical, and in every possible respect, the exact sort of *scene*—attention-seeking in every way—that he hated.

And oh, would he hate this.

There were only two days left before he came back by the time she was done. So she settled in, enjoyed the bold, silly freedom of the place while she could, and tried to get ready for the coming storm.

CHAPTER NINE

AT FIRST VALENTINO thought that he must be having a stroke. A cardiac event of some kind. The first strange note was that none of his staff would meet his eye. He noticed it when his man met him in the drive, as he always did. And instead of exchanging the usual polite few words, he had simply tended to the luggage and hustled away.

But it did not take more than two steps into his house to understand why.

First he assumed he was dying. Or had died. He was not sure which was preferable.

Nor did he need anyone to tell him what had happened here. He could put it together.

She had transformed the house into…a cacophony. There was no other word for it.

"Yes," came her voice, and he realized that he'd said the word out loud, having followed the explosion of color on top of color, next to pattern and more color, all the way down the great hall and back. "It is a great, glorious cacophony of emotion. Behold it. Learn to love it. That's what it's for."

Valentino took his time turning to look at this woman.

This madwoman who he had married, who was sitting on his steps like a wild creature someone must have dragged in from the sea. Her hair looked as if it hadn't seen a brush since he'd left. Somehow it looked redder and thicker and much, much wilder, an impression she was helping along by being barefoot. Though it was nearly December and despite the sunny days, it was not warm. She otherwise wore paint-splattered overalls and some kind of torn shirt beneath them. Like an urchin instead of the wife of one of the richest men alive and a princess in her own right.

But what he couldn't seem to look away from was that defiant look on her face.

"And what," he asked in as calm a voice as he could manage, which was perhaps not very calm at all, "did you imagine my response would be to this outrage?"

"I hoped, of course, that you would see it as the gift that it is," Carliz replied, almost *merrily*, to his ear. "But if you can't, then I think it's a reasonable enough trade." When he stared at her without comprehension, she smiled. "You do not wish me to express my emotions, Valentino. So you can look at them."

The strangest part was that he was not as irate, as awash in fury, as he should have been. He should have been cut straight through by this act of destruction when he had told her exactly what this house meant to him in its pristine state. This time he had been betrayed by his wife, who claimed to love him just as others had— and Valentino clearly needed to take a hard look at why there was such a long line of these betrayals throughout his life.

But as he stared at her, what he regretted was not that he had essentially handed her the means to strike at him like this by ordering her to fit in with the house. But that he had not taken her along with him on his trip.

It reminded him of that vow he'd made himself right after the wedding. He had wondered who, exactly, he had been trying to teach a lesson. Because Carliz was not only the one woman he could not forget, she was also the only person he could not tuck away into an appropriate compartment, never to think of again.

She was a curse. If his trip had been a test, he had failed it. Has he been as haunted by her in all the hotels he'd been forced to stay in, in all the cities he'd visited, as he was here.

Maybe that was why he did not react the way he might have even ten days ago. He did not lecture her. He did not attempt to order her to do this or that.

Instead, he looked at the colors. At the shapes and images. And it was a bit of a shock to see that she was actually a good artist when he'd thought her interest in art was that of a dilettante. If he was a different sort of man, he might consider this house a masterpiece and congratulate himself for giving her the perfect canvas.

But he was the man he'd been fashioned into right here on this island.

And it was time she understood that this was not a game he was playing.

"Very well done," he told her. The weariness of travel seemed to fall away the more he gazed at her, but there was a cure for that. He was about to show her. "If you're so visual that you felt the need to deface every surface of my home, then perhaps you should see for yourself."

She looked intrigued. He had known she would. "Tell me more."

He lifted a brow toward her...costume. "You will need to dress in something that does not make you look like a street urchin I swept up on my way back. Like some kind of dust mite."

"My darling man," she said, with that laugh he did not wish to admit that he had missed. But there the truth of it was. He had missed it. "I am the Princess Royal of Las Sosegadas. If I start appearing in public dressed like an urchin, everyone else will, too."

All the same, she went and she changed her clothes and when she came down she looked breathtakingly, simply sophisticated. Precisely as he'd known she would.

And that was when he took her to see his father.

It was faster to drive to his father's house, but he wanted to make all of his points as best he could. He wanted to make sure she fully understood him.

Because one thing he understood, now that he had seen what she'd done to his house—a perfect example of what she'd been doing to him, for years down—was that he had lost. Whatever fight this was, whatever strategy he'd imagined he could employ to gain the upper hand, it had all come to nothing.

She had won.

And so all that was left to him was to show her precisely what it was she could claim as her prize. What she had to look forward to. What would become of the pair of them, thanks to this insistence of hers on haunting him wherever he went.

He blamed himself. Of course he did. He had turned out to be exactly the kind of man he'd always sworn he would transcend.

But first, he walked with her.

"Many stories have been told about this island," he said as he led her out behind the house and onto a path that led away from the hill and its view over the water, up along the cliffs. "No one believes that anyone in my family is related to the most famous bearer of our surname, though there have been many ideas about who else we might have been. All that is known for certain is that the island was the province of goat herders for a long while, as it is of no strategic importance to anyone. And eventually, it came into the possession of one of my ancestors. It is said the ancestor in question was particularly beguiled by the island's pastoral charm."

"It is a rare island that does not have some or other charms."

Carliz walked beside him, seeming to keep pace with him effortlessly despite the increasing roundness of her form. She had gotten even bigger while he'd been away, and it amazed him that it suited her. All this *ripeness*.

When he glanced at her now, she wasn't looking at him. Her gaze was out on the water, watching the way the late fall light danced over the waves, silver and gold at once. She had tamed the bohemian he'd seen on his stairs quickly. Her hair was now twisted back into a knot on her head that looked nothing short of sophisticated. What she was wearing was not in itself extraordinary.

A pair of trousers cut beautifully, boots that gripped the uneven path beneath them, and a sweater wrapped around her that looked at least as soft as cashmere, the better to keep out the chill of the ocean air.

Though all around him, the island smelled like cinnamon instead of salt.

"You are a chameleon," he said.

She laughed at that, and the look she shot his way was appraising. "I'm going to choose to take that as a compliment. I think."

"You seem to fit in wherever you go, effortlessly."

"Not effortlessly," she corrected him. "It's supposed to look that way though. I'm glad it does." Carliz seemed to feel his frown on the side of her face and when she looked over to confirm it, she made another low noise. "I was about to say that you should know this, but there's no reason you should. Your family has its measure of fame and notoriety, but it isn't the same as mine. Being a member of a royal family isn't the same thing as being famous. Or even notorious. We are public property, no matter what sort of monarchy it is that we belong to. And so every interaction requires public service, in one form or another. My sister and I were taught from a very young age that there was very little as important as making everyone around us feel comfortable. She is actually better at it than me, but you wouldn't know it."

"She's too lofty, then?"

Carliz shook her head. "That's not what I meant at all. It's only that she's the queen, you see. So no matter how hard she works to make people comfortable around her, what they see is *the queen*. Nonetheless, practicing being effortless is the bulk of what we did growing up. I think other children played. We practiced."

He walked on and the fact that they were next to a cliff with a terrible drop to the rocks below did not escape his notice. He thought it was fitting. He had spent the whole of his life vowing that he would not be like his mother. That he would not be like any other member of his family, in any regard. And here he was all the same.

Wrecked as surely as if he had tossed himself over the side.

A threat his mother had liked to make with regularity.

"There was only one person in my family who ever seemed effortless," Valentino said, though he had to force himself to say these words. He had spent so long *not* saying them. "And by that, I mean he was effortlessly cruel. He took pleasure in everyone else's pain. After my mother died, he only got worse. And over time, it became clear to me that my brother's reckless charm, as I have heard it called, was modeled directly on his. I vowed that I would be like neither of them. That I would honor those who came before me instead."

"You mean your mother?"

"I mean my grandparents, who deserved a far better son than the one they got." He blew out a breath, not liking that even talking of these things made him feel...not himself. All jangly and rough inside. "I have done my best to fill that gap, or so I thought. And then, instead, I allowed myself to get embroiled with you."

"Well and truly embroiled," she said, sounding perfectly cheerful.

"I'm trying to explain myself to you," he told her

darkly, everything in him…in a terrible kind of pain he could not begin to name. "This does not come easily."

"What you are doing, Valentino, is walking along a cliff in late November, making dark mutterings that never quite come to the point," she said. Gently enough, though there was a thread of something like exasperation beneath, to his ear. "Remember, you didn't save me any pain these last few years. You caused it. Pretending this wasn't happening didn't make it go away. It just made it hurt more."

"That was not my intention."

"But it's what happened." She shrugged as if it was nothing. "Lucky for you, I love you anyway."

"Why?" he bit out. "Why have you been so certain, all along?"

She looked at him curiously. "Because I saw you," she said, as if it was simple. "I looked across a ballroom in Rome and there you were. I saw you. I recognized you. I knew you." She shrugged. "I can't explain it."

And she didn't even wait for his reaction to that, or look for it. That was how comfortable she was with the words. The sentiments themselves. He thought of all those bold shapes and bright colors, on every surface. Demanding that he see.

But she simply kept talking. "And now look. Despite all of that, here we are anyway."

"Yet I am the only one who knows where we really are," he told her. "You will understand shortly."

She did not reply to that cryptic remark. They walked further, just over the next rise, and then he pointed. Down below, down a narrow set of stairs cut into the side of the hill, was the stretch of land his father liked to call The Peninsula. It was a relatively narrow bit of rock and sand that stuck out from the top of the island, and it was the site of the first house. Now it was known as Bonaparte's Folly, which was an apt a name as any, Valentino supposed.

"Welcome to hell," he said darkly.

He did not mean that to be amusing. So he was surprised when beside him, Carliz laughed.

And she was still laughing as she started for the stairs, gliding down them in a light-footed sort of way that made it clear she had no idea what she was getting herself into.

But that was the point of this, he reminded himself. His father was always issuing summons, Valentino only occasionally responded to them, and that was how they'd been banging along for ages now. Left to his own devices, he didn't think he would respond at all, but anytime he leaned in that direction, Milo had a terrible habit of showing up at the worst possible times. And for the express purpose of embarrassing his son.

His revenge, Valentino knew. Because he did not like to be ignored.

At the bottom of the stairs, Carliz was already marching for the house that stood there, dark and imposing like all the nightmares he'd had as a child. He had to hurry to catch up with her, and when he did, she only tossed him a look and kept going.

"I'm not afraid of your father," she told him.

Valentino ran a hand through his hair, a childhood tell he'd thought he'd beaten out of himself long since.

"I'm not afraid of him either. But I don't underestimate how good he is at what he does, either."

"I understand." She kept her eyes on the house before them, a true antique building that had been updated only in parts—those parts being the bits of the house his father liked. The rest of the old pile could fall off into the sea for all he cared. Mind you, he still held on to every heirloom, every painting, every bit of the heritage the house contained, because he knew that worrying about how casually he might destroy it kept Valentino up at night.

"I don't think you do understand," he gritted out to Carliz as they walked. "But you will."

She stopped then, just short of the grand entrance. "My father was in no way the devil. I loved him dearly. But I was a disappointment to him and he told me so. And because he told me those things when I was very young, very impressionable, I have given them an undue weight over the rest of my life."

He only stared back at her, certain he did not know what she meant. And even more certain that he did not wish to know.

"But I have come to understand that all of us choose our own shadows," she told him, her treasure chest eyes locked to his. "Just as we choose our own pleasures. They are ours to pick through, discard, or carry forever. We decide."

"You will see," he told her, filled with prophecy and doom—and that same pain beneath. "There is a reason my father lives on an island, instead of in the center of a glittering city. He has a habit of repelling almost everyone he comes into contact with. It's better by far if he remains in seclusion."

"Excellent," she said, and her lips curved in a way that really made him wish he had not come here with her. It made him wish that he had expressed his feelings on the topic of paint selection and artistic license in the manner they both enjoyed most, but it was too late. The die was cast. He could already hear stirrings from inside. "I've always wanted to ask a hermit what exactly it is they do all day. Sort through their thoughts? Tell themselves stories, as if a stuck on a desert island? I've always wondered if they think less or more than other people while all alone."

"My father thinks of only one thing," Valentino told her as the locks on the door were thrown, locks Milo had ostentatiously put there to lock them all in when Valentino's mother's behavior was at its worst. He kept them, all these years later, as an immediate reminder of those turbulent years. The screaming, the fighting. Broken glass and sobbing into the morning. "How to be the center of attention in all things."

Then the door was thrown open, and there stood Milo himself.

Smiling affably.

Valentino had often thought that one of life's great injustices was that his father did not resemble the kind of person he was inside. Because if he did, he would be gnarled and pockmarked and ridden with marks, poisoned from the inside out. Instead, he stood tall, with a full head of thick, dark hair. He was a vain man, and policed the lines on his face, comparing his looks to anyone he considered an enemy—which was to say, everyone he'd ever met. He was also partial to staring at his sons and despairing, loudly, that they should have received the great bounty of his genes while giving him so little in return.

As if their mothers had not been involved at all.

Milo was not as tall as either Valentino or Aristide. Valentino thought he got shorter every time they met, though maybe that was only wishful thinking on his part.

Though he would have seen them coming from one of his many windows, Milo took the time to stare at Valentino as if his appearance was a surprise. His lip curled, and Valentino could see the spark that usually preceded one of his cutting remarks in the light of his eyes.

But he didn't say a word. He only turned his attention to Carliz, because he thought that the only reason a beautiful woman existed was to admire him.

And because he was likely hoping it would provoke Valentino.

Yet what Valentino felt was what he had when he was young, when he'd *known* that it was somehow his fault his mother was trapped on the island. Forced to live with Milo because of Valentino. Because Valentino was born, she was imprisoned.

It was possible she might have said so herself on some of her less lucid evenings.

He had tried to put himself between his mother and Milo, so he could protect her. And it had taken him most of his life to understand that she had not wanted protection. Not his. Not anyone's. What she'd wanted was attention. Milo's attention, specifically.

But she'd never cared how she got it.

Nonetheless, he was grown now and Carliz was his wife, not his mother. And he knew too well that not only would his father take far too much of a delight in it if he betrayed his usual composure by trying to take fire for her—but Carliz herself would not like it.

Milo still stood in the doorway, blocking it, his gaze moved insultingly over Carliz's entire body. Up, then down, and then back again to focus on her round belly.

Valentino thought his jaw might break, he was clenching it so hard.

"Well, well, well," Milo murmured, making a meal of it all in that odious tone of his. It dripped like acid down Valentino's spine. "How nice of our famous party girl princess to drop by and say hello to someone so unimportant as her husband's only blood relative. Full blood relative I mean."

Valentino had made a mess of all of this. He understood that more keenly now than ever. He had let himself do the precise thing he'd known he could never do, not without ending up like his poor, lost mother—strung out on passion, destroyed by claims of love.

But he did not like the way his father was looking at his wife. Any more than he liked the way Milo made that distinction in their blood, as if Aristide wasn't Milo's full blood relation as well.

Most of all he hated the fact that he could see straight through his father, and yet the man's relentless nastiness worked all the same.

But before he could say or do anything, or haul Carliz out of here before she was poisoned too, she laughed.

That absurd confection of a laugh that she was rightly famous for. This was one of the ways she sparkled hither and yon, all over the globe, like a mirror ball.

"I'd be tempted to take exception to that," she said as the laughter faded, reaching out and tapping Milo on the arm as if he was standing there telling a set of jokes. As if they were friends. "But I'm not the type that takes against a friendly bit of hazing amongst family. Especially when I'm sure you know better, Signor Bonaparte."

Milo's eyes flattened. "I know a great many things, as a matter-of-fact."

She leaned in like she was telling him a secret. "Then you know. You can call me *Your Royal Highness*."

And it was the way she said it. As if she was extending an invitation—suggesting that he remember himself while also making fun of her exalted station. Nothing could possibly have fascinated and infuriated Milo more. It was masterful. And she wasn't afraid, this marvel of a wife of his. She was completely assured.

She was Carliz of Las Sosegadas and she knew her own magnificence.

He did, too. Because he had seen her, recognized her. He had known her from that very same moment in Rome. Valentino stopped trying to pretend otherwise.

Even though they were here, where that kind of thing was used for sport. To hunt down any foolish enough to show it.

Carliz let out that laugh again, as if she was gracing

Milo with a joke of her own. She even gave him a conspiratorial smile, showing him nothing but what she likely wanted him to see—the Princess Royal in all her glory. As unafraid as ever. Of Milo, but also of Valentino. Of this thing between them he would still rather deny. "It has a much better ring, don't you think?"

CHAPTER TEN

MILO BONAPARTE WAS a pig.

There was no prettying that up. There was no lipstick that would make the man anything but what he was. Tiny. Venal.

And vicious, as men like him always were. He'd tried to put her down, she'd pulled rank, and now he would not rest until he found a better way to get that scorpion's sting deep into her flesh. She'd met far too many men like Milo in her day. She'd learned long ago that it was best to laugh along, never quite seeming to get that he wasn't joking, and then to beat a quick retreat as soon as possible.

"Spicy," Milo said, taking her arm and standing too close. "I like it."

Carliz laughed. "A little spice goes a long way," she said, and then launched into an artless anecdote about accidentally eating too many Pot Douglah peppers in Trinidad on a silly trip one year.

She laughed and she laughed and she put space between her and Milo, but her heart ached for Valentino, who could not have done the same kinds of things when he was a child. He must have felt trapped here, battered this way and that by his father's cruelties.

Because Milo, like all other men of his ilk, liked nothing so much as a captive audience. That much was obvious.

And he was making a meal of it today. He took his *new princess-in-law*, as he insisted on calling her, all around the old castle as if conducting a tour. What he was really doing, Carliz was aware, was sticking any knife he could think of in deep so that Valentino would squirm.

Valentino did not give him the satisfaction. Externally. But if she could see that he held himself more stiffly than usual, she was certain that Milo saw it too.

So she found herself going full social butterfly. After all, this was one of the things she had always been good at. Drawing fire so that the real target—usually her sister—could get some breathing room. Because it didn't matter what this man thought. She didn't care what he thought. To her, he was nothing but another small, disappointing specimen who had an undue influence on the man she'd fallen in love with.

"There used to be flower beds all along the side of the house," Milo said in his oily way as they passed a set of windows. "They were ugly. I had them removed."

Carliz suspected that the flower beds were a sore point, because Valentino's jaw looked like granite. "What a shame," she replied, with another laugh. "I've always thought that as flowers can only ever be lovely, any fault in them must be down to maintenance."

And before Milo could tell her what—who—he was

talking about, she set off on a circuitous story about the year she'd spent wandering from one major flower show to the next, from Philadelphia to Melbourne to Singapore and to Chelsea. She raved on about orchids until Milo walked ahead of her, likely to drown her out.

"They were my mother's favorite flowers," Valentino said in a low voice, looking at her with an expression on his face that made her heart hurt. "They died from neglect, but he likes to pretend he took them down himself. In the end, I suppose it doesn't matter how he killed them."

"It matters," she whispered back, fiercely. "It all matters."

Eventually, after a tour through the portrait gallery in which Milo lingered over a portrait of Valentino's mother and Carliz had made certain to act as if she was incapable of taking any negative bit of the story on board, he led them into a sitting room. He insisted they sit. Then he rang for service.

With a malicious sort of glimmer in his gaze.

They all sat there in a fraught sort of silence, until a beautiful older woman arrived at the door. She began silently serving them coffees and biscotti. Home baked, clearly.

But what fascinated Carliz was the way the woman looked at Valentino. With something like longing. Or perhaps it was regret.

Whatever it was, Valentino did not meet her gaze.

Carliz knew this was the famous housekeeper—Aristide's mother, Ginevra—the one who would not leave Milo's employ. No matter what was said about her. Or him, for that matter.

The one who had taught Valentino how to cook.

Clearly pleased with the interplay, no matter how silent, Milo settled back with his coffee and beamed.

The visit did not improve from there.

By the time they left—by the time, that was, that Valentino shot to his feet in the middle of one of his father's sly, insulting monologues wrapped up in the pretense of an actual conversation, he had managed to cover a lot of ground.

"He managed to insult not only my sister and her reign *and* the whole of my country, but both of my parents, one of whom has been dead for some time." Carliz said it wonderingly as they climbed back up the steep stairs, both of them breathing deep as if they'd been slowly suffocating to death in that house. She wasn't quite laughing, but she wasn't *not* laughing, either. It was all so vile and relentless. "I was either so beautiful that it made me an automatic whore or not quite beautiful enough to keep the eye of a Bonaparte, I couldn't tell. It kept going back and forth. And I do believe, right there at the end, that when he started going on about the apple only falling from the tree if the fruit is rotten straight through, that he was actually propositioning me."

"He was."

Valentino's voice was grim, but Carliz was too busy climbing stairs and putting distance between her and that man to pay close attention to that. "Really, if you step back and think about it, the whole thing was a pitiful work of art. Such comprehensive and contradictory insults piled one on top of the next. I've never seen the like."

"You shouldn't have had to suffer through it now."

They made it to the top of the stairs and she pulled her soft cardigan closer around her, because it had gotten colder. She kept forgetting that it would do that, given the boundless sunshine of most days. It wasn't like the mountains, where the change of seasons did not require any interpretation. And it certainly wasn't as cold here as it would be at home.

But even she was not immune, no matter how alpine her blood, to the wind right off an ocean that cut straight to the bone.

Valentino seemed impervious to the cold because of whatever was burning in him. She looked at him, then stopped walking herself. Because he looked if something inside him had *ignited*.

And not in the way she liked best.

"I hope you see, now," he growled at her when he had her attention. "No matter what I do, no matter where I go, there's always *that*. I always come back to that room. That man. That psychodrama that we have all been playing our parts in since I was born."

She felt stunned by that. Winded. "Valentino. I don't know what you thought was happening. But it's not you who should be apologizing for any of that behavior."

"The better he knows a person, the worse it gets," Valentino said, as if she hadn't spoken. "He finds their weaknesses. He exposes them, and capitalizes on them. He is relentless. Day after day, year after year."

"He is the voice in your head," Carliz said softly, as

it occurred to her that they had somehow found themselves on uncertain ground again. "I'm sorry for that."

And when he looked at her then, he looked wild and untethered. Not like the controlled Valentino she'd seen so much of, and something in her shook at that.

"My mother and my father together were a disaster," he told her roughly. "And I have dedicated my life to making certain that I will never reenact that disaster, Carliz. I told you. Again and again, I told you that this could never be anything. I tried to keep you safe from it. You would not listen."

She felt something begin to shake, deep inside her. She found herself wrapping her arms around her own body, as if she could keep it in. Or as if she could make it better, somehow, by not letting him see that any of this was upsetting her.

But even as she thought that, she thought that really, that was the problem. All this pretending things didn't hurt when they did. All of this pretending not to feel when that was about as effective as pretending not to breathe.

She had loved him from the very first second she'd seen him. She had acted on that ever since. He knew that she had. Why was she bothering to *pretend*?

So she blew out a breath, and she watched him take note of the fact that it came out shuddery. "No," she agreed. "I would not listen. And do you know why?"

"Because you did not understand what you are dealing with," he thundered at her. He swept arm out toward the peninsula. Toward that sad little house that stood there, weathering storms inside and out. "This is me being honest with you, Carliz. Brutally, totally honest in the only way I can, and you still can't accept the truth."

She studied him, something beating too hard inside her. Some kind of low, desperate panic, because she didn't like the sound of his honesty. She didn't like the look on his face.

"You mean more honest than pretending the only thing between us is sexual?" she asked.

"That is the only thing that we can indulge in."

He moved closer and then his hands were on her upper arms, pulling her toward him. And surely there was something deeply twisted in her that she should revel in that. Exult in it. Yet she had known, so long ago in Rome and with one glance, that this man could fit her so well. That he could speak to every single part of her as well as he did. Even now, that knowing was like a rock inside her, and everything else was built on it.

And she also knew that if she did not fight for what she wanted now, he would roll right over her in his determination to pretend none of this was happening between them. The way he always did. She lifted her hands and slid them onto his chest, not precisely to push him away. But it was not welcoming, either.

"I met your father," she said, evenly. Very evenly. "And he seems like a lonely, bitter old man, who like many lonely, bitter old men, thinks it a great laugh to antagonize anyone who draws near. I don't know why you would imagine that he has anything to do with you. Or us."

"Because this is my blood!" he cried out, as if in anguish. "This is who I am. I've done my best to be something else, Carliz. Anything else. You have no idea how hard I've tried. I've tried so hard to be a good man. To walk the path of the honorable in every way. To do my best to live up to my grandfather's example, with dignity. And instead I am reduced to nothing more than...*this*."

"Is *this* so bad?" she asked, softly. She searched his face, his hard jaw. "What do you think would happen if you stopped trying to hide yourself from me, Valentino? What would happen if you did something truly remarkable, like taking me out to dinner? If we sat in a restaurant, ordered food, and talked to each other as if we were simply...people?"

"Why can't you see?"

And he sounded so wounded. She felt for him, truly she did. If she could have, she would have taken this pain away from him.

But there was more to think of here than his feelings, whether he would admit he had them or not.

Carliz knew a little bit about the things families passed down, one generation to the next, even with the best of intentions. Heirs and spares. Good ones and bad ones. The roles people played that had never quite fit them, but they couldn't seem to shed. The expectations that sat heavy, like the weight of crowns.

She wanted better than that for her child. Maybe every mother did.

Maybe, a voice inside suggested, *your mother does too. Maybe that's what all her picking and picking is about. Maybe you've been reading it wrong, all this time.*

"If you let this man destroy your marriage the way he destroyed his," Carliz said, as gently as she could when her heart was breaking. "Don't you see? Then he's winning. You're letting him win."

Valentino stared down at her and she could see all the different faces he had shown her, whether on purpose or not. That stranger she'd seen so unexpectedly in Rome. How startled he looked. How shocked, just as she had been.

That grief she'd seen on his face in that drafty old castle keep. The unbearable weight of it all.

Her stern, deliciously hard lover, who knew no boundaries he could not push and cajoled her into heights she could not even have imagined, before him.

The bleak look on his face now. An echo of the way he had looked at her at their wedding. And that morning in July when he'd told her that they would never see each other again.

But now, here, standing on top of the cliff as the wind got colder and harsher, she saw everything. What he had been trying to hide. What she had been letting him hide. Because none of this—nothing between them—occurred in a vacuum.

"My father was a monster," Valentino bit out in that same rough tone. "He let my mother die because she had ceased to amuse him. The only reason my brother and I are alive is because it entertains him to have us forever at each other's throats."

"Then why not defy him and become the best of friends," she asked, trying to sound cool and remote but failing. "After all, who has more in common with you than Aristide? Who but the two of you know how you were raised, what happened here, and what you must carry in the wake of it?"

He shook his head at that, as if she'd delivered a body blow. "You can't reason with a monster like my father, Carliz. And I have always known that I have the same monster in me. Look at how I treat you. Look at what I think passes for desire. For passion."

"You mean those things we do *together*?" This time she laughed in disbelief, and a sharper hurt than she would have thought possible. "Those things you taught me? That I treasure?"

"I'm as twisted as he is," Valentino intoned, handing down a pronouncement from on high. "And it does not matter how I try to compartmentalize this obsession I have for you. I know where it ends. I watched it end terribly once already. I cannot allow myself to do the same thing. Carliz. Please. Listen to me when I tell you that whatever poisoning him is in me, too. It's the same blood. It only ends up in the same place."

And they were both breathing too hard then. There were too many things swirling around in her head. All the things she could say. All the things she felt.

But instead, she moved closer, tipping her face up to his, not caring at all when the rain began to fall.

"We are standing at a crossroads, you and I. A literal one. If you look down to your left, you'll see your past. In a stone house on the end of a spit of land, waiting for the sea to take it back." It was almost as if they might kiss, wildly, impossibly. It felt like that, but darker, while they were so close. So still. So *ravaged* by these things that he thought owned him. "On your right is the house you built so you could control it. So you could keep it stark and cold, because you thought that would keep you safe."

"It was never about safety," he argued. And he wasn't lying. She could see that. He believed that it had been about those things he'd told her it was about. *Calm. No scenes.* He didn't understand that all of that was the same fear.

"But I have defaced it, Valentino," she said, low and urgent. "It is bright now. Filled with color and chaos, and surely you must know that soon enough, there will be a child there too. And he will not follow your commands. He will not do as he is told. He will cry and he will disrupt our sleep and he will not care who you are or what promises you made to yourself long ago." She tapped on the chest before her, not gently. "He will want his father, and so you have to choose. It's that stark. The darkness or the light, but the choice has to be yours."

"You think it's a crossroads. You think it's a choice." He was shaking his head, but he didn't let go of her arms. "But all these things are in me, all of the time. It doesn't matter what I choose, they will all come with me. And soon enough..."

"Soon enough, what?" she demanded, and maybe there were tears in the corners of her eyes. Maybe not only in the corners, but slipping out and joining the raindrops that gathered there as the winter weather moved in, but she didn't bother to dash them away. "What is the point of you going to such lengths to have control over everything in the world if you don't have control of yourself? If you're worried about snapping, Valentino, there is a solution. *Don't.*"

He heaved out a breath. "As if it's that simple."

"You forget that I've met your father," she countered, pressing her palms into the wall of his chest. "Do you really believe that he's faced with some kind of internal moral dilemma? He's not. I don't know if that makes it better or worse. He didn't *accidentally* become the way he is, my love. He likes it. He *wants* to be cruel. If you don't, if that's not who you are… *You don't have to be anything like him.*"

She was not sure she had ever said anything more intently in all her life.

"I want desperately to believe that," Valentino told her in a gravelly voice. "But deep inside me, a voice always reminds me—"

"That's *his* voice!" she cried at him.

Then she stepped back, because she was too close to using the one weapon they both wielded so expertly, and with such deadly effect. Because she knew that if she kissed him here, they would consummate this moment, whatever it was, out here in the rain, the wind. And it would be glorious. She would come apart so thoroughly that she would think for a moment that it was impossible she might ever be put back together.

She loved that feeling almost beyond reason.

But then she would come back into her body, hard.

And everything would be exactly the same.

So she backed away. And she didn't care any longer if he saw her tears. If he saw her shake.

She was either able to show what she felt or she wasn't. There was no sense hiding it.

"You think that this is an honorable thing that you're doing," she said then, though everything in her shouted at her to move toward him. To taste him. To hold on to him any way she could. It hurt that she didn't. "You think that if you cut yourself off from emotion, from feeling anything—even though you already feel it—you can avoid it. Control it. But that's a lie, Valentino. And you might be able to lie to yourself. But don't you understand by now? You've never been any good at lying to me. Because I know that what you feel is real. I've always known. I don't know how."

But she did. It was that same chain, linking them together. She could almost see it gleaming now, out here in all this wet.

He said her name, or she thought he did, but the rain stole the sound away from him.

Carliz kept going. "And pretending otherwise doesn't make you a hero. It makes you a coward. And if you act like this? If this is the life you choose?" She put one hand on her belly, and with her free one she pointed right at him. "Sooner or later, your son will see you for the liar and the coward you are, and then what will you be to *him*? Just another monster, like your father is to you?"

The rain came down. The wind whipped at them. She thought he might have made a noise, the sort of noise an animal might make while in pain. And she hated herself for causing him pain.

But that didn't mean what she said was in any way untrue.

So she stepped back, still holding his gaze, no matter it was rain slicked too.

"Your choice, Valentino," she whispered, and she knew he heard her.

The rain and the wind could only take so much.

Then she turned around, though everything in her protested. She forced herself back along the cliffs and then down into the house she'd painted all those bright colors. It seemed a lifetime ago.

And even now, even after she'd faced his monster of a father and come out none the worse for wear, he didn't want to love her.

Carliz had to look at it head-on. She took herself, dripping wet and rapidly growing cold, and toweled off. She wrapped herself in every blanket she could find and curled up on the chaise in her favorite sitting room.

She stared at the wall she'd painted bright yellow and blue, and hung with old paintings. And she asked herself what—exactly—she planned to do for herself and her child if Valentino couldn't love them the way he should.

Because she might have decided it was enough to know what she knew, to have that faith. But she couldn't ask the same of her child. And that meant she would have to leave him.

Carliz didn't know how she was going to make herself do that, again.

Or how she thought she was going to live without him.

CHAPTER ELEVEN

VALENTINO STAYED OUT in that storm for a long time.

Every word she'd said hit hard and pounded into him, like hail.

One stone after the next, each one of them hitting their mark with deadly accuracy.

Was that his father's voice inside of him, that dark sneering thing that was so quick to point out his failures?

He thought of his family's history and all of those things he'd always taken as fact. Because he felt them himself? Or because his father had known what he felt and had steered him one way or the next as it suited him?

Had his brother betrayed him? Had his father made it seem as if *he* had betrayed his brother?

Maybe Carliz was right to point out that the true act of defiance would have been to stay friends with Aristides. The only true friend he'd ever had. They had adored each other.

His father hadn't liked that, had he?

And something else occurred to him, then. Was it possible that there was something critical he was missing when it came to love, to feelings, that Ginevra showed every day—by choosing to remain in a place she could have left? By choosing to love as she chose, no matter if it was returned. No matter what anyone else thought.

No matter if it was love or penance or something more complicated, it was hers. And she did not shy away from it.

And Ginevra had been a good mother not only to her son, but to Valentino, too. Little as he might have understood that at the time.

He thought of the kind of mother Carliz already was, and how different that was than his own. Because she had been so fragile, so consistently precarious, his poor mother. She had been so unable to fight her own demons, much less the man who'd married her so that he could toy with them too.

She had never stood a chance against Milo.

Then again, she also hadn't tried.

That truth seemed to hit him like lightning.

Because there was no way that his father could have done the extent of the damage on his wife if she'd been a woman like Carliz. It simply would not have happened.

First she would have laughed. Then she would have left.

And she most certainly would have taken her child with her.

Something in him seemed to grow warmer and brighter at that thought. And then, the more he held on to it, it was as if something inside him began to melt.

And as it melted, he felt seized with what he could only call a tidal wave of the kind of emotion he never allowed himself.

Not openly. It had to be sex, and specifically the kind of sex he controlled. It had to be the rules he made. The life he lived.

That was his emotion. That was how he *felt*.

But she'd known all along, hadn't she?

And as it broke over him, he began to run. Through the rain, through the gathering dark. He catapulted himself down the side of the cliff and raced through the gardens, desperate to get there.

He made it to the door and threw it open.

Because inside, there was color. Inside, it was bright and warm and happy.

And Carliz was here.

Since the moment he had laid eyes on her in Rome, she had been a bright, hot light leading him home.

Little as he had wished to accept that.

He ran through the house, shouting her name, not caring at all that his servants looked at him in astonishment.

He shouted again and again, until she appeared wrapped once more in what looked like a selection of scarves—

Except these were not chosen to seduce.

These were blankets, and if he was not mistaken, she'd chosen them to hide.

Something about the notion of his vibrant, gloriously bright Carliz hiding herself away made him ache. This house was already a monument to her vulnerability, painted in bold strokes so there could be no mistaking it.

She had made his house into a masterpiece to show him her love, and he had delivered her to a monster.

It was time to rectify this situation, once and for all.

Valentino walked up the stairs, aware of every brush-stroke as he passed. The color here, the competing color there. She had told him the story of her love, of their love, and he had rewarded her by telling her that a stone house of misery was their future instead.

When he got to the top of the stairs he stared at her for a wordless moment, and then he simply dropped to his knees.

She made a startled sort of sound, or perhaps it was a sob. The blankets fell all around them as she reached out to take his face between her hands.

Carliz gazed down at him as if she wanted to soothe him, even now.

"I looked up across a standard, boring event, and was hit by lightning," he told her, hoping she could hear that he was speaking from his heart. Hoping she could see it on his face. Or even hear the way his heartbeat was threatening his ribs. "You know exactly what my life was like. It was this house. Beautiful in its way, but cold. Deliberately empty. Stark and studied. And then there you were. With your hair too many colors and your eyes too wise and knowing, and you saw me. And I looked at you and I saw nothing but color."

She moved closer, and whispered something, but he knew he had to get these things out. Because he was tired, so tired, of the things he'd kept deep inside.

The things that had hurt them both.

"Later I would say you were a witch. That I was com-pelled against my will, but I wasn't. You are so *bright*. I wanted to get close to you. I wanted to see if it was pos-sible that anything could warm me the way you looked as if you could, and then you did." He gazed up at her. "I think I started melting then, and I've been fighting it ever since, and Carliz, I want that love story I've been reading about in the papers for years. I want to love you so much and so well that strangers pick up on it in a crowded room that I wasn't even in. I want to make you happy, and I understand what an extraordinary thing that is to say. I don't think I have ever been happy a day of my life unless you were beside me. And even then, I did my best to ruin it. But I want it all the same."

"The good news," she managed to say, her voice rough and her eyes shining, "is that we did vow to stay together forever. So we have some time to practice."

Something in him eased then, little though he understood what she was doing. He had expected to find her packing. He had expected her to show him coldness. He had expected—

But he got it, then.

She loved him. This was love. She was forgiving him in real time. She was showing him what it was like when someone was truly in love with him.

It wasn't easy. It might even hurt. But the love never stopped.

The love was like that light of hers, and it shone on forever.

"You could not have made anything more clear to me," he forced himself to say, to keep going, because that must be love too. Because that was what she did, What she had done and was still doing. "Than when you told me that I was set to become to my own son the very father who has worked so hard to ruin my life. So this is my other vow to you, while it is still just us."

Though it wasn't. Not really. Their baby was there between them. He smoothed his hands over her belly, filled with awe and reverence, as always.

And love, he understood at last.

All of this was love.

"I will love you," he whispered to the child she carried. *His son.* "I will not use you as some kind of sick entertainment that only I enjoy. I will try to raise you to be a good man, freed from the kind of voices I carry around inside me. And I promise you, I will not be a monster."

Carliz winced. "I didn't mean that."

But Valentino smiled. "You did. And you were right."

He stood then, pulling her close so he could smooth his hands over that wild hair of hers, let loose again from the knot she'd tied it in. Then he wiped away the moisture beneath her eyes, carefully, as if every tear was precious.

"I love you," she whispered.

"*Mia principessa*, then there is no time to waste. We have already wasted too much time. You must know that I have always loved you. You have told me you knew it. And I intend to love you forever, as best I can, and I..." But he paused, then. His heart pounded against his ribs. "I want to start over. If, of course that is what you want." And he realized, in this moment, how strong she was. How courageous to paint her bleeding, broken heart all over this house When he could hardly bear to ask a simple question. "Is it, Carliz? Can we start again, you and I?"

And for a moment, she looked something like dazed.

But then a smile broke over her face, brighter by far than any of the paint she'd slapped on his walls. Better than the brightest, sunniest day.

"Valentino," she said, smiling so wide he found himself smiling too, as if that was something he did with regularity—though he thought perhaps he should, "I thought you'd never ask."

CHAPTER TWELVE

THEY DID EXACTLY THAT.

They started over, as if they were new.

As if both of them were ready to accept what had happened that night in Rome, then and there.

And it was good.

But it was one thing to thunder on to his wife and spend his days relearning every part of her so that he might love her better.

Other relationships required more care.

He met with his brother in the Diamond Club, some weeks before Christmas.

"It's almost as if you're stalking me," Aristide said in his usual droll way. "And to think, you had to come all the way to London to do it when, last I checked, we were neighbors."

"I'm having a son," Valentino said. Starkly. He made no attempt to dress it up, and because his brother looked taken aback by that, he continued. "I would like him to know his cousins. I would like him to have the run of the island, as we did. And play as we did. And know nothing at all about our father or what came before. I wish we could have had that longer than we did."

Aristide sat in the seat opposite Valentino, and gestured for his whiskey. He waited for a staff member to produce a glass, tossed it back, and then sat a moment before he spoke.

"If I didn't know better," he said, mildly, "I might begin to suspect that this is your version of an apology."

Valentino smiled. Then he leaned forward, and held his brother's gaze. "I would like to think of it as a new beginning." But because he was no longer playing the role he had for so long, he smiled. "If that is something you would find yourself amenable to."

And he found himself something a little too close to choked up when his brother looked at him, cleared his throat as if there was emotion there too, and then nodded.

When he told Carliz the story, she cried.

She cried a lot throughout the rest of her pregnancy. They spent most of their time on the island, though he would often whisk her away to this city or that. He would take her out to dinner at the finest restaurants, where they would sit. And order food off menus. And talk of everything and nothing.

"Look at us," she said after one such meal, her hand threaded with his as they walked back through the lively streets of Barcelona. "We seem just like *people*."

"Or near enough, Your Royal Highness," he murmured.

Their son was born entirely perfect in every way, not that they were biased. And they liked him so much that they decided to give him a set of brothers, three in total. He taught them how to be decent men and kept them away from his father. Carliz taught them perfect manners and her own dry wit, and encouraged them to run like wild animals all over the island with their cousins.

Just the way he and Aristide had done when they were small.

Life was good, because they made it good. Valentino learned to splash about in color. And how to love Carliz the way she deserved.

That it turned out, was the easiest part of all.

It was loving himself, too, that took work. It was the mirror that intimacy held up to his own true face that gave him pause.

But then, there were cures for that.

His children's delight in him, so different from the fear he'd felt for his own father. Or the sick need he'd had to protect his mother when he'd been too young to understand what was going on.

And when they were alone, the games that he played with his wife when both of them were naked, that these days were all about correction, not control.

Life was good. They made sure of it.

As the years passed, even a monster like Milo could not talk his way out of mortality. And it was a truth worth learning early that people died how they lived. Once the old man was gone, the brothers came together and knew that neither one of them could or would ever live in that house again.

"I suppose we can't burn it down," Aristide said, regretfully.

Valentino was tempted to light the match himself. "It does have historic value."

So they decided to make it something far better than it had ever been during their father's lifetime. An orphanage, but one that would take care of children instead of degrading and diminishing them.

One that would lift them up instead of smashing them down.

And it turned out, despite everything, that Valentino Bonaparte made himself into a good man instead of a monster. With the great honor of a life lived, if not always as well as he'd like, as fully as he could. With the legacy of mended fences with his brother and a set of cousins who would never know that there had ever been any distance between their parents.

Best of all, he had Carliz to walk with him all along the path, sharing it all with him. Every step. Every moment. Making it better simply because she was there. All of that laughter. All of that joy. All because of one night in Rome and the brightest light he'd ever seen, guiding him home.

A home they made together, from scratch and brand-new, every morning they woke up and started again.

Which they planned to do forever.

And did.

* * * * *

Were you captivated by Pregnant Princess Bride?
Then don't miss the other installments in
The Diamond Club series!

Baby Worth Billions
by Lynne Graham

Greek's Forbidden Temptation
by Millie Adams

Italian's Stolen Wife
by Lorraine Hall

Heir Ultimatum
by Michelle Smart

His Runaway Royal
by Clare Connelly

Reclaimed with a Ring
by Louise Fuller

Stranded and Seduced
by Emmy Grayson

Available now!